Romeo and Juliet

William Shakespeare

About William Shakespeare:

William Shakespeare was an English poet, playwright, and actor, widely regarded as the greatest writer in the English language and the world's greatest dramatist. He is often called England's national poet and the "Bard of Avon" (or simply "the Bard"). His extant works, including collaborations, consist of some 39 plays, 154 sonnets, two long narrative poems, and a few other verses, some of uncertain authorship. His plays have been translated into every major living language and are performed more often than those of any other playwright.

Shakespeare was born and raised in Stratford-upon-Avon, Warwickshire. At the age of 18, he married Anne Hathaway, with whom he had three children: Susanna and twins Hamnet and Judith. Sometime between 1585 and 1592, he began a successful career in London as an actor, writer, and part-owner of a playing company called the Lord Chamberlain's Men, later known as the King's Men.

At age 49 (around 1613), he appears to have retired to Stratford, where he died three years later. Few records of Shakespeare's private life survive; this has stimulated considerable speculation about such matters as his physical appearance, his sexuality, his religious beliefs, and whether the works attributed to him were written by others.

Shakespeare produced most of his known works between 1589 and 1613. His early plays were primarily comedies and histories and are regarded as some of the best work produced in these genres. Until about 1608, he wrote mainly tragedies, among them Hamlet, Othello, King Lear, and Macbeth, all considered to be among the finest works in the English language. In the last phase of his life, he wrote tragicomedies (also known as romances) and collaborated with other playwrights. Many of Shakespeare's plays were published in editions of varying quality and accuracy in his lifetime. However, in 1623, two fellow actors and friends of Shakespeare's, John Heminges and Henry Condell, published a more definitive text known as the First Folio, a posthumous collected edition of Shakespeare's dramatic works that included all but two of his plays. The volume was prefaced with a poem by Ben Jonson, in which Jonson presciently hails Shakespeare in a now-famous quote as "not of an age, but for all time".

Throughout the 20th and 21st centuries, Shakespeare's works have been continually adapted and rediscovered by new movements in scholarship and performance. His plays remain popular and are studied, performed, and reinterpreted through various cultural and political contexts around the world.

Romeo and Juliet Study Guide:

Romeo and Juliet, Shakespeare's most famous tragedy and one of the world's most enduring love stories, derives its plot from several sixteenth century sources. Shakespeare's primary inspiration for the play was Arthur Brooke's Tragical History of Romeus and Juliet (1562), a long and dense poem. Brooke's poem, in turn, was based on a French prose version written by Pierre Boiastuau (1559), which was derived from an Italian version written by Bandello in 1554. Bandello's poem, meanwhile, was an interpretation of Luigi da Porto's 1525 version of a story by Masuccio Salernitano (1476).

The plot of Shakespeare's Romeo and Juliet remains mostly true to Brooke's poem, though Shakespeare exercised artistic license in several instances. For example, as he often does, Shakespeare telescopes the events from Brooke's poem (which took place over 90 days) into a few days in the play. Additionally, Shakespeare's Juliet is thirteen, while Brooke wrote her as sixteen. The time compression and the younger Juliet enhance the youthful nature of the central relationship, emphasizing its passion and newness.

One of the most powerful aspects of Romeo and Juliet is Shakespeare's use of language. The characters curse, vow oaths, banish each other, and, in general, demonstrate great verbal dexterity through an overuse of action verbs. In addition, the play is saturated with oxymorons, puns, paradoxes, and double entendres. Shakespeare even calls the use of names into question, most famously in Juliet's balcony soliloquy. Shakespeare also executed a rather strong shift in the language spoken by both Romeo and Juliet after they fall in love. Whereas Romeo is hopelessly normal in his courtship before meeting Juliet, after he falls in love, his language becomes infinitely richer and stronger.

Romeo and Juliet also deals with the issue of authoritarian law and order. Many of Shakespeare's plays feature characters that represent the unalterable force of the law, such as the Duke in The Comedy of Errors and Prince Escalus in Romeo and Juliet. In this play, the law attempts to stop the civil disorder, and even banishes Romeo at the midpoint. However, as in The Comedy of Errors, the law is eventually overpowered by the forces of love.

There are several different sources that inform the contemporary text of Romeo and Juliet. Romeo and Juliet was first published in quarto in 1597, and republished in a new edition only two years later. The second copy was used to create yet a third quarto in 1609, from which both the 1623 Quarto and First Folio are derived. The first quarto is generally considered a bad quarto, or an illicit copy created from the recollections of several actors rather than from the writer's original material. The second quarto seems to be taken from Shakespeare's rough draft, and thus has some inconsistent speech and some lines which Shakespeare apparently meant to eliminate. Please see the "About Shakespearian Theater" section of this note for more guidance as to these concepts.

Romeo and Juliet was popular during Shakespeare's time, but over the centuries it has become nothing short of omnipresent. It is arguably the most-filmed play of all time, and has been adapted 4 times to date - first by George Cukor in 1936, then by Franco Zeffirelli in 1968, Baz Luhrmann in 1996, and most recently, by Carlo Carlei in 2013. John Madden's Academy-Award winning film Shakespeare in Love is a fictional account of Shakespeare's life while writing the play. It was the basis for Prokofiev's famous ballet, and has inspired numerous Operas, pop and jazz songs, books, games, and musicals.

Romeo and Juliet Summary

Romeo and Juliet is set in Verona, Italy, where there is a progressing quarrel between the Montague and Capulet families. The play opens with hirelings from the two houses occupied with a road fight that in the end attracts the family patriarchs and the city authorities, including Prince Escalus. The Prince parts of the bargains giving a declaration that restricts any further battling at the danger of incredible discipline.

In the interim, Romeo, a youngster from the Montague house, mourns his solitary love for a lady named Rosaline, who has pledged to stay modest for an amazing remainder. Romeo and his companion Benvolio happen to discover a Capulet hireling, Peter, who is attempting to peruse a rundown of invitees to a veiled gathering at the Capulet house that night. Romeo assists Peter with perusing the rundown and chooses to go to the gathering on the grounds that Rosaline will be there. He intends to wear a cover so he will no one will remember him as a Montague.

Romeo shows up at the Capulets' gathering in ensemble. He becomes hopelessly enamored with youthful Juliet Capulet from the minute he sees her. Be that as it may, Juliet's cousin Tybalt perceives Romeo and needs to slaughter him on the spot. Master Capulet intercedes, demanding that Tybalt not upset the gathering since it will outrage the Prince. Resolute, Romeo discreetly approaches Juliet and admits his affection for her. In the wake of trading adoring words, they kiss.

A while later, Juliet's Nurse discloses to Romeo that Juliet is a Capulet, which disturbs the stricken youth. In the interim, Juliet is likewise upset when she discovers that Romeo is a Montague. Soon thereafter, Romeo climbs the nursery divider into Juliet's nursery. Juliet rises on her gallery and talks her private musings so anyone can hear. She wishes Romeo could shed his name and wed her. After hearing her admission, Romeo shows up and discloses to Juliet that he adores her. She cautions him to be valid in his adoration, and he depends on his own self that he will be. Before they part, they concur that Juliet will send her Nurse to meet Romeo at nine o'clock the following day, so, all things considered he will set a spot for them to be hitched.

The Nurse completes her obligation, and advises Juliet to meet Romeo at the sanctuary where Friar Laurence lives and works. Juliet meets Romeo there, and the Friar weds them stealthily.

Benvolio and Mercutio (another of Romeo's companions) are looking out for the road soon thereafter when Tybalt shows up. Tybalt requests to know where Romeo is with the goal that he can move him to a duel, so as to rebuff him for sneaking into the gathering. Mercutio is articulately unclear, yet Romeo happens to show up in the center of the verbal competing. Tybalt challenges him, however Romeo latently opposes battling, so, all things considered Mercutio bounces in and draws his sword on Tybalt. Romeo attempts to hinder the two men, however Tybalt removes Mercutio and runs, just to return after he hears that Mercutio has kicked the bucket. Irate over his companion's passing, Romeo battles with Tybalt and murders him. At that point, he chooses to escape. At the point when Prince Escalus shows up at the homicide scene, he expels Romeo from Verona for eternity.

The Nurse reveals to Juliet the miserable news about what has happened to Tybalt and Romeo. Juliet is heart-broken, yet she understands that Romeo would have been slaughtered on the off chance that he had not battled Tybalt. She sends her Nurse to discover Romeo and give him her ring.

That night, Romeo sneaks into Juliet's room, and they perfect their marriage. The following morning, he is driven away from when Juliet's mom shows up. Romeo goes to Mantua, where he trusts that somebody will send news about Juliet or his expulsion.

During Romeo and Juliet's just night together, in any case, Lord Capulet concludes that Juliet ought to wed a youngster named Paris, who has been requesting her hand. Master and Lady Capulet tell Juliet of their arrangement, yet she won't, angering her dad. At the point when both Lady Capulet and the Nurse won't mediate for the young lady, she demands that they walk out on her.

Juliet then visits Friar Laurence, and together they create an arrangement to rejoin her with Romeo. The Friar gives Juliet a mixture that will cause her to appear to be dead for at any rate two days, during which opportunity Romeo will come to meet her in the Capulet vault. The Friar vows to send expression of the arrangement to Romeo.

Juliet drinks the Friar's mixture that night. The following morning, the day of Juliet and Paris' wedding, her Nurse discovers her "dead" in bed. The entire house criticizes her suicide, and Friar Laurence demands they rapidly place her into the family vault.

Tragically, Friar John has been not able to convey the letter to Romeo educating him regarding the arrangement, so when Romeo's hireling acquires him news Mantua that Juliet has kicked the bucket, Romeo is heart-broken. He rushes back to Verona, on the whole, purchases poison from an Apothecary and composes a suicide note itemizing the terrible course of occasions. When Friar Laurence understands that his letter never made it to Romeo's hands, he races to the Capulet tomb, wanting to show up before Romeo does.

Romeo shows up at the Capulet vault and thinks that it's watched by Paris, who is there to grieve the loss of his pledged. Paris provokes Romeo to a duel, and Romeo murders him rapidly. Romeo at that point conveys Paris' body into the grave and puts it down. After observing Juliet's "dead" body lying in the tomb, Romeo drinks the toxic substance, gives her a last kiss - and bites the dust.

Monk Laurence shows up to the vault similarly as Juliet awakens. He attempts to persuade her to escape, yet after observing Romeo's dead body, she ends her own life also.

The remainder of the town begins to show up at the tomb, including Lord Capulet and Lord Montague. Minister Laurence clarifies the entire story, and Romeo's letter affirms it. The two families consent to settle their fight and structure a collusion regardless of the unfortunate conditions.

Character List:

Romeo

Sixteen-year-old Romeo Montague falls in love with Juliet Capulet at a masquerade, thus igniting their tragic affair. Romeo is defined by a self-indulgent melancholy at the beginning of the play, but later becomes a much more active and committed character, which is clear when he kills Tybalt. Romeo's final act of passion is when, believing his beloved Juliet is dead, he takes his own life. Throughout the play, Romeo embraces an idealistic view of love, which explains why he falls for Juliet so quickly and passionately.

Lord Montague

Romeo's father and a mortal enemy of the Capulets.

Lady Montague

Romeo's mother, who dies from a broken heart after Romeo is banished from Verona.

Benvolio

Romeo's cousin, and a staunch pacifist.

Abram

A Montague serving man involved in the street brawl in 1.1.

Balthazar

Romeo's servant, who is involved in the street fight of 1.1, and later assists Romeo in the final Act.

Friar Laurence

An older man and a friend to Romeo. He officiates the wedding of Romeo and Juliet, hoping to gain political peace through the union. When that doesn't work out, he concocts the plan to reunite the star-crossed lovers by giving Juliet a sleeping potion - but the plan backfires.

Juliet

Juliet Capulet is a thirteen-year-old girl who falls in love with Romeo Montague. She has a strong will and a rebellious streak - she knows what she wants. Defined by a shrewd intelligence and pronounced agency, Juliet is in many ways a more masculine character than Romeo is, even if the patriarchy of her family limits her power. Her final decision to kill herself speaks to her pronounced focus and commitment.

Lord Capulet

Juliet's father and a temperamental bully who initially pretends to consider his daughter's welfare while arranging her marriage, but later demands her quick union with Count Paris. Her father's pressure is a catalyst in the final sequence of events that ends in Juliet's suicide.

Lady Capulet

Juliet's mother is submissive to her husband, and refuses to intercede for Juliet when their daughter expresses concern over the arranged marriage to Count Paris.

Tybalt

Juliet's hot-headed cousin, whose penchant for violence leads to the Act III street fight - ending in his own death as well as Mercutio's.

Nurse

Juliet's nurse is ostensibly the young girl's confidante, but also harbors a certain amount of resentment that makes her useless when it comes to saving the girl. Nurse often makes trouble for Juliet by refusing to give her information quickly, and later turns into a traitor by arguing Juliet should marry Paris, even though she knows about her secret marriage to Romeo.

Peter

A Capulet serving man who serves as great comic relief in Act I when he is unable to read the list of invitees to the Capulet ball.

Sampson

A Capulet serving man who is involved in the street brawl in 1.1.

Gregory

A Capulet serving man who is involved in the street brawl in 1.1.

Prince Escalus

The ruler of Verona who provides for and represents law and order in the city. He frequently attempts to cede the violence between the Montagues and Capulets, but he finds himself powerless against true love.

Mercutio

Romeo's friend, a kinsman of the Prince, and one of the play's most colorful characters. In the early Acts, Mercutio displays a pronounced wit and colorful language. However, by Act III, as he lies dying after the street fight, he delivers a damning speech on the feuding houses. Mercutio's death marks the play's turn into tragedy.

Paris

Count Paris is Juliet's suitor - Lord Capulet supports the union but Juliet despises him. Though never as insidious as Lord Capulet, Paris behaves arrogantly once the marriage date is set. He confronts Romeo in Act V, which leads to the Count's death in battle.

Apothecary

Shakespeare describes the apothecary of Mantua as a skeleton - so he appears to personify Death itself. A poor man, he is easily convinced to sell Romeo the poison that he uses to kill himself.

Citizens of the Watch

These unspeaking characters often arrive at the scene of a street brawl, representing the forces of law and order that combat the disorder wrought by the family feud.

Romeo and Juliet Themes

Love

In spite of the fact that Romeo and Juliet is ostensibly the most model romantic tale in the English language, it depicts just a quite certain sort of affection: youthful, nonsensical, enthusiastic love. In the play, Shakespeare at last recommends that the sort of affection that Romeo and Juliet feel drives sweethearts to institute a narrow minded seclusion from their general surroundings. Romeo and Juliet shun their duties to any other person, deciding to act benevolently just towards each other. Sexuality pervades the play, both through ribald jokes and in the way that Romeo and Juliet envision culminating their marriage, yet it doesn't characterize their affection. Rather, their energetic desire is one of numerous reasons why their relationship becomes so serious so rapidly. All through the play, Shakespeare just depicts Romeo and Juliet's adoration as a transient eruption of young energy. In a large portion of his work, Shakespeare was progressively keen on investigating the sparkles of fascination than long haul duty. Taking into account that no different connections in the play are as unadulterated as that among Romeo and Juliet, however, it is anything but difficult to see that Shakespeare regards the intensity of such an energetic, enthusiastic love yet additionally mourns its short life.

Passing

In Romeo and Juliet, passing is all over. Indeed, even before the play moves in tone after Mercutio's demise, Shakespeare makes a few references to death being Juliet's groom. The danger of brutality that swarms the principal demonstrations shows itself in the last 50% of the play, when key characters pass on and the main darlings approach their horrible end. There are a few manners by which the characters in Romeo and Juliet think about death. Romeo endeavors suicide in Act III as a demonstration of weakness, yet when he searches out the Apothecary in Act V, it is an indication of solidarity and solidarity. The Chorus sets up the story's sad end toward the start of the play, which hues the crowd's understanding from the beginning - we realize that this energetic, honest love will end in catastrophe. The structure of the play as a catastrophe from the earliest starting point makes Romeo and Juliet's affection considerably increasingly appalling on the grounds that the crowd knows about their approaching passings. The excursion of the play is the cycle from affection to death - and that is the thing that makes Romeo and Julie so enduring and amazing.

Age

All through Romeo and Juliet, Shakespeare sets up the ideological gap that frequently isolates adolescents from grown-ups. The characters in the play would all be able to be arranged as either youthful, energetic characters or more established, increasingly utilitarian characters. The young characters are solely characterized by their vitality and lack of caution – like Romeo, Juliet, Mercutio, and Tybalt. In the interim, the more seasoned characters all view the world as far as governmental issues and practicality. The Capulet and Montague patriarchs are positively feisty contenders, however think regarding triumph as an idea, overlooking the potential enthusiastic cost of their quarrel. Minister Laurence, who apparently speaks to Romeo and Juliet's inclinations, sees their association as far as its political result, while the youthful darlings are just worried about fulfilling their quickly pulsating hearts. While Shakespeare doesn't place a good to the partition among youthful and old, it shows up all through the play, proposing that the negativity that accompanies age is one of the numerous reasons that people definitely breed hardship among themselves. It additionally verifiably gives motivation to youthful sweethearts to try to isolate themselves from a 'grown-up' universe of political brutality and trading.

Personality

Romeo and Juliet recommends that people are frequently hamstrung by the personalities constrained upon them from outside. Most outstandingly, this subject is show in Juliet's overhang discourse, in which she asks, "Goodness Romeo, Romeo, wherefore workmanship thou Romeo?" (2.1.75). The focal hindrance of the play is that the two enthusiastic darlings are isolated by a quarrel dependent on their family names. The way that their affection has little to do with their given characters makes no difference to their general surroundings, thus they should decide to shun those personalities while they are as one. Sadly, this demonstration of dismissal likewise implies Romeo and Juliet must disregard the world outside their agreeable case, and, therefore, the savage powers eventually crash downward on them. A solid feeling of personality can positively be an aid throughout everyday life, except right now, just powers partition between the characters. Indeed, even Mercutio, who isn't really a Montague, is murdered for his relationship with that family. The liveliest characters in Romeo and Juliet bite the dust not in view of what their identity is, but since of the names that the outside world has

Retribution

Romeo and Juliet recommends that the longing for vengeance is both a characteristic and an overwhelming human quality. From the minute that the play spirals towards calamity in Act III, the vast majority of the horrible occasions are started by retribution. Tybalt searches out Romeo and murders Mercutio from a half-cooked want for retribution over Romeo's participation at the disguise ball, and Romeo executes Tybalt to retaliate for Mercutio. Romeo's craving for vengeance is overwhelming to such an extent that he doesn't interruption to consider how his assault on Tybalt will bargain his ongoing union with Juliet. Obviously, the fundamental set-up of the play is dependent upon a long-standing quarrel between the Montagues and Capulets, the reason for which does not make any difference anymore. The only thing that is in any way important is that these families have kept on avenging overlooked insults for ages. In spite of the fact that Shakespeare seldom, if at any point, lectures, Romeo and Juliet positively presents vengeance as a silly activity that consistently causes more mischief than anything.

Marriage

In Romeo and Juliet, Shakespeare doesn't paint an alluring image of the establishment of marriage. The main positive depiction of marriage – between the main darlings – must be directed covertly, and even Friar Laurence marginally opposes in light of the fact that Romeo and Juliet have chosen to marry so rapidly. Shakespeare is by all accounts recommending that marriage dependent on unadulterated love doesn't have a place in a world that mishandles the holy association. The way where Lord Capulet demands Juliet's union with Paris recommends both the manner in which he sees his little girl as item and the manner by which marriage can fill in as a weapon against an insubordinate young lady. Indeed, even the strict figure, Friar Laurence, considers union with be political; he weds Romeo and Juliet to pick up the political force end the quarrel between their families, and not on the grounds that he fundamentally affirms of their adoration. At last, the focal marriage in Romeo and Juliet finishes in death, indicating that this sort of energetic, nonsensical association can't exist in a world energized by detest and vengeance.

THE PROLOGUE

Enter Chorus.

Chor. Two households, both alike in dignity,
in fair Verona, where we lay our scene,
from ancient grudge break to new mutiny,
where civil blood makes civil hands unclean.
From forth the fatal loins of these two foes
A pair of star-cross's lovers take their life;
Whose misadventur'd piteous overthrows
Doth with their death bury their parents' strife.
The fearful passage of their death-mark'd love,
And the continuance of their parents' rage,
Which, but their children's end, naught could remove,
Is now the two hours' traffic of our stage;
The which if you with patient ears attend,
What here shall miss, our toil shall strive to mend.
[Exit.]

Summary

The chorus introduces the play and establishes the plot that will unfold. They explain how two families in Verona – the Capulets and the Montagues - have reignited an ancient feud, and how two lovers, one from each family, will commit suicide after becoming entangled in this conflict. These lovers are Juliet Capulet and Romeo Montague. Only after the suicides will the families decide to end their feud.

ACT I. Scene I. Verona. A public place.

Enter Sampson and Gregory (with swords and bucklers) of the house of Capulet.

Samp. Gregory, on my word, we'll not carry coals.

Greg. No, for then we should be colliers.

Samp. I mean, an we be in choler, we'll draw.

Greg. Ay, while you live, draw your neck out of collar.

Samp. I strike quickly, being moved.

Greg. But thou art not quickly moved to strike.

Samp. A dog of the house of Montague moves me.

Greg. To move is to stir, and to be valiant is to stand. Therefore, if thou art moved, thou runn'st away.

Samp. A dog of that house shall move me to stand. I will take
the wall of any man or maid of Montague's.

Greg. That shows thee a weak slave; for the weakest goes to the
wall.

Samp. 'Tis true; and therefore women, being the weaker vessels,
   are ever thrust to the wall. Therefore I will push Montague's men
   from the wall and thrust his maids to the wall.

Greg. The quarrel is between our masters and us their men.

Samp. 'Tis all one. I will show myself a tyrant. When I have fought with the men, I will be cruel with the maids- I will cut off their heads.

Greg. The heads of the maids?

   Samp. Ay, the heads of the maids, or their maidenheads.
   Take it in what sense thou wilt.

Greg. They must take it in sense that feel it.

   Samp. Me they shall feel while I am able to stand; and 'tis known I
   am a pretty piece of flesh.

   Greg. 'Tis well thou art not fish; if thou hadst, thou hadst
   been poor-John. Draw thy tool! Here comes two of the house of
   Montagues.

Enter two other Servingmen [Abram and Balthasar].

Samp. My naked weapon is out. Quarrel! I will back thee.

Greg. How? turn thy back and run?

Samp. Fear me not.

Greg. No, marry. I fear thee!

Samp. Let us take the law of our sides; let them begin.

Greg. I will frown as I pass by, and let them take it as they list.

Samp. Nay, as they dare. I will bite my thumb at them; which is disgrace to them, if they bear it.

Abr. Do you bite your thumb at us, sir?

Samp. I do bite my thumb, sir.

Abr. Do you bite your thumb at us, sir?

Samp. [aside to Gregory] Is the law of our side if I say ay?

Greg. [aside to Sampson] No.

Samp. No, sir, I do not bite my thumb at you, sir; but I bite my thumb, sir.

Greg. Do you quarrel, sir?

Abr. Quarrel, sir? No, sir.

Samp. But if you do, sir, am for you. I serve as good a man as you.

Abr. No better.

Samp. Well, sir.

Enter Benvolio.

Greg. [aside to Sampson] Say 'better.' Here comes one of my master's kinsmen.

Samp. Yes, better, sir.

Abr. You lie.

Samp. Draw, if you be men. Gregory, remember thy swashing blow.
> They fight.

Ben. Part, fools! [Beats down their swords.]
Put up your swords. You know not what you do.

Enter Tybalt.

Tyb. What, art thou drawn among these heartless hinds?
Turn thee Benvolio! look upon thy death.

Ben. I do but keep the peace. Put up thy sword,
Or manage it to part these men with me.

Tyb. What, drawn, and talk of peace? I hate the word
As I hate hell, all Montagues, and thee.
Have at thee, coward! They fight.

> Enter an officer, and three or four Citizens with clubs or
> partisans.

Officer. Clubs, bills, and partisans! Strike! beat them down!

Citizens. Down with the Capulets! Down with the Montagues!

Enter Old Capulet in his gown, and his Wife.

Cap. What noise is this? Give me my long sword, ho!

Wife. A crutch, a crutch! Why call you for a sword?

  Cap. My sword, I say! Old Montague is come
  And flourishes his blade in spite of me.

Enter Old Montague and his Wife.

Mon. Thou villain Capulet!- Hold me not, let me go.

M. Wife. Thou shalt not stir one foot to seek a foe.

Enter Prince Escalus, with his Train.

  Prince. Rebellious subjects, enemies to peace,
  Profaners of this neighbour-stained steel-
  Will they not hear? What, ho! you men, you beasts,
  That quench the fire of your pernicious rage
  With purple fountains issuing from your veins!
  On pain of torture, from those bloody hands
  Throw your mistempered weapons to the ground
  And hear the sentence of your moved prince.
  Three civil brawls, bred of an airy word
  By thee, old Capulet, and Montague,
  Have thrice disturb'd the quiet of our streets
  And made Verona's ancient citizens
  Cast by their grave beseeming ornaments
  To wield old partisans, in hands as old,
  Cank'red with peace, to part your cank'red hate.
  If ever you disturb our streets again,
  Your lives shall pay the forfeit of the peace.
  For this time all the rest depart away.

You, Capulet, shall go along with me;
And, Montague, come you this afternoon,
To know our farther pleasure in this case,
To old Freetown, our common judgment place.
Once more, on pain of death, all men depart.
          Exeunt [all but Montague, his Wife, and Benvolio].

Mon. Who set this ancient quarrel new abroach?
Speak, nephew, were you by when it began?

Ben. Here were the servants of your adversary
And yours, close fighting ere I did approach.
I drew to part them. In the instant came
The fiery Tybalt, with his sword prepar'd;
Which, as he breath'd defiance to my ears,
He swung about his head and cut the winds,
Who, nothing hurt withal, hiss'd him in scorn.
While we were interchanging thrusts and blows,
Came more and more, and fought on part and part,
Till the Prince came, who parted either part.

M. Wife. O, where is Romeo? Saw you him to-day?
Right glad I am he was not at this fray.

Ben. Madam, an hour before the worshipp'd sun
Peer'd forth the golden window of the East,
A troubled mind drave me to walk abroad;
Where, underneath the grove of sycamore
That westward rooteth from the city's side,
So early walking did I see your son.
Towards him I made; but he was ware of me
And stole into the covert of the wood.

  I- measuring his affections by my own,
  Which then most sought where most might not be found,
  Being one too many by my weary self-
  Pursu'd my humour, not Pursuing his,
  And gladly shunn'd who gladly fled from me.

 Mon. Many a morning hath he there been seen,
  With tears augmenting the fresh morning's dew,
  Adding to clouds more clouds with his deep sighs;
  But all so soon as the all-cheering sun
  Should in the furthest East bean to draw
  The shady curtains from Aurora's bed,
  Away from light steals home my heavy son
  And private in his chamber pens himself,
  Shuts up his windows, locks fair daylight
  And makes himself an artificial night.
  Black and portentous must this humour prove
  Unless good counsel may the cause remove.

Ben. My noble uncle, do you know the cause?

Mon. I neither know it nor can learn of him

Ben. Have you importun'd him by any means?

 Mon. Both by myself and many other friend;
  But he, his own affections' counsellor,
  Is to himself- I will not say how true-
  But to himself so secret and so close,
  So far from sounding and discovery,
  As is the bud bit with an envious worm
  Ere he can spread his sweet leaves to the air
  Or dedicate his beauty to the sun.
  Could we but learn from whence his sorrows grow,

We would as willingly give cure as know.

Enter Romeo.

Ben. See, where he comes. So please you step aside,
I'll know his grievance, or be much denied.

Mon. I would thou wert so happy by thy stay
To hear true shrift. Come, madam, let's away,
Exeunt [Montague and Wife].

Ben. Good morrow, cousin.

Rom. Is the day so young?

Ben. But new struck nine.

Rom. Ay me! sad hours seem long.
Was that my father that went hence so fast?

Ben. It was. What sadness lengthens Romeo's hours?

Rom. Not having that which having makes them short.

Ben. In love?

Rom. Out-

Ben. Of love?

Rom. Out of her favour where I am in love.

Ben. Alas that love, so gentle in his view,
Should be so tyrannous and rough in proof!

Rom. Alas that love, whose view is muffled still,
Should without eyes see pathways to his will!
Where shall we dine? O me! What fray was here?
Yet tell me not, for I have heard it all.
Here's much to do with hate, but more with love.
Why then, O brawling love! O loving hate!
O anything, of nothing first create!
O heavy lightness! serious vanity!
Misshapen chaos of well-seeming forms!
Feather of lead, bright smoke, cold fire, sick health!
Still-waking sleep, that is not what it is
This love feel I, that feel no love in this.
Dost thou not laugh?

Ben. No, coz, I rather weep.

Rom. Good heart, at what?

Ben. At thy good heart's oppression.

Rom. Why, such is love's transgression.
Griefs of mine own lie heavy in my breast,
Which thou wilt propagate, to have it prest
With more of thine. This love that thou hast shown
Doth add more grief to too much of mine own.
Love is a smoke rais'd with the fume of sighs;
Being purg'd, a fire sparkling in lovers' eyes;
Being vex'd, a sea nourish'd with lovers' tears.
What is it else? A madness most discreet,
A choking gall, and a preserving sweet.
Farewell, my coz.

Ben. Soft! I will go along.
An if you leave me so, you do me wrong.

Rom. Tut! I have lost myself; I am not here:
This is not Romeo, he's some other where.

Ben. Tell me in sadness, who is that you love?

Rom. What, shall I groan and tell thee?

Ben. Groan? Why, no;
But sadly tell me who.

Rom. Bid a sick man in sadness make his will.
Ah, word ill urg'd to one that is so ill!
In sadness, cousin, I do love a woman.

Ben. I aim'd so near when I suppos'd you lov'd.

Rom. A right good markman! And she's fair I love.

Ben. A right fair mark, fair coz, is soonest hit.

Rom. Well, in that hit you miss. She'll not be hit
With Cupid's arrow. She hath Dian's wit,
And, in strong proof of chastity well arm'd,
From Love's weak childish bow she lives unharm'd.
She will not stay the siege of loving terms,
Nor bide th' encounter of assailing eyes,
Nor ope her lap to saint-seducing gold.
O, she's rich in beauty; only poor
That, when she dies, with beauty dies her store.

Ben. Then she hath sworn that she will still live chaste?

Rom. She hath, and in that sparing makes huge waste;
For beauty, starv'd with her severity,
Cuts beauty off from all posterity.

She is too fair, too wise, wisely too fair,
To merit bliss by making me despair.
She hath forsworn to love, and in that vow
Do I live dead that live to tell it now.

Ben. Be rul'd by me: forget to think of her.

Rom. O, teach me how I should forget to think!

Ben. By giving liberty unto thine eyes.
Examine other beauties.

Rom. 'Tis the way
To call hers (exquisite) in question more.
These happy masks that kiss fair ladies' brows,
Being black puts us in mind they hide the fair.
He that is strucken blind cannot forget
The precious treasure of his eyesight lost.
Show me a mistress that is passing fair,
What doth her beauty serve but as a note
Where I may read who pass'd that passing fair?
Farewell. Thou canst not teach me to forget.

Ben. I'll pay that doctrine, or else die in debt. Exeunt.

Summary

Two Capulet hirelings – Sampson and Gregory – linger in the city, sitting tight for some Montague workers to pass. They chat, utilizing sexual allusion and unrefined jokes to kid about ladies, and talk with enmity about the Montagues. They regret that the law disallows battling, and wonder how to begin a fight lawfully.

At the point when the Montague workers – Abram and Balthasar – show up, Sampson nibbles his thumb at them (which is discourteous however not illicit). Offended, Abram stands up to Sampson and a battle starts.

Benvolio, Romeo's cousin, shows up to find the battle in progress. Drawing his sword, he orders them to stop. At that point, Tybalt, Juliet's cousin, strolls onto the road. After observing his opponent, Benvolio, Tybalt additionally draws his sword, reigniting the fight.

Ruler Capulet – the patriarch of the family – shows up at the fight, and requests a sword with the goal that he may participate. Be that as it may, Lady Capulet controls him, considerably after Lord Montague develops prepared to battle.

For reasons unknown, the Citizens of the Watch have spread expression of the road battle, and Prince Escalus shows up before anybody is executed. The Prince scolds the Montagues and the Capulets for their shared hostility, which he accepts is making the lanes of Verona perilous. The Prince at that point orders everybody to get back and stop threats at the danger of incredible discipline. He actually goes with the Capulets home.

The Montagues and Benvolio stay in front of an audience. The family asks Benvolio where Romeo is, and he reveals to them that the kid has been feeling bizarre recently. At the point when a serious Romeo at long last shows up, the Montagues solicit Benvolio to decide the reason from his despairing, after which they leave.

When Benvolio gets some information about the wellspring of his despair, Romeo clarifies that he is pining for a lady named Rosaline, who intends to stay modest for a mind-blowing remainder. This lonely love is the reason for Romeo's downturn.

Scene II. A Street.

Enter Capulet, County Paris, and [Servant] -the Clown.

Cap. But Montague is bound as well as I,
In penalty alike; and 'tis not hard, I think,
For men so old as we to keep the peace.

Par. Of honourable reckoning are you both,
And pity 'tis you liv'd at odds so long.
But now, my lord, what say you to my suit?

Cap. But saying o'er what I have said before:
My child is yet a stranger in the world,
She hath not seen the change of fourteen years;
Let two more summers wither in their pride
Ere we may think her ripe to be a bride.

Par. Younger than she are happy mothers made.

Cap. And too soon marr'd are those so early made.
The earth hath swallowed all my hopes but she;
She is the hopeful lady of my earth.
But woo her, gentle Paris, get her heart;
My will to her consent is but a part.
An she agree, within her scope of choice
Lies my consent and fair according voice.
This night I hold an old accustom'd feast,
Whereto I have invited many a guest,

    Such as I love; and you among the store,
    One more, most welcome, makes my number more.
    At my poor house look to behold this night
    Earth-treading stars that make dark heaven light.
    Such comfort as do lusty young men feel
    When well apparell'd April on the heel
    Of limping Winter treads, even such delight
    Among fresh female buds shall you this night
    Inherit at my house. Hear all, all see,
    And like her most whose merit most shall be;
    Which, on more view of many, mine, being one,
    May stand in number, though in reck'ning none.
    Come, go with me. [To Servant, giving him a paper]
Go,
    sirrah, trudge about
    Through fair Verona; find those persons out
    Whose names are written there, and to them say,
    My house and welcome on their pleasure stay-
               Exeunt [Capulet and Paris].

Serv. Find them out whose names are written here? It is written that the shoemaker should meddle with his yard and the tailor with his last, the fisher with his pencil and the painter with his nets; but I am sent to find those persons whose names are here writ, and can never find what names the writing person hath here writ. I must to the learned. In good time!

Enter Benvolio and Romeo.

  Ben. Tut, man, one fire burns out another's burning;
    One pain is lessoned by another's anguish;
    Turn giddy, and be holp by backward turning;
    One desperate grief cures with another's languish.
    Take thou some new infection to thy eye,

And the rank poison of the old will die.

Rom. Your plantain leaf is excellent for that.

Ben. For what, I pray thee?

Rom. For your broken shin.

Ben. Why, Romeo, art thou mad?

Rom. Not mad, but bound more than a madman is;
Shut up in Prison, kept without my food,
Whipp'd and tormented and- God-den, good fellow.

Serv. God gi' go-den. I pray, sir, can you read?

Rom. Ay, mine own fortune in my misery.

Serv. Perhaps you have learned it without book. But I pray, can you read anything you see?

Rom. Ay, If I know the letters and the language.

Serv. Ye say honestly. Rest you merry!

Rom. Stay, fellow; I can read. He reads.

'Signior Martino and his wife and daughters;
County Anselmo and his beauteous sisters;
The lady widow of Vitruvio;
Signior Placentio and His lovely nieces;
Mercutio and his brother Valentine;
Mine uncle Capulet, his wife, and daughters;
My fair niece Rosaline and Livia;
Signior Valentio and His cousin Tybalt;
Lucio and the lively Helena.'

[Gives back the paper.] A fair assembly. Whither should they
  come?

Serv. Up.

Rom. Whither?

Serv. To supper, to our house.

Rom. Whose house?

Serv. My master's.

Rom. Indeed I should have ask'd you that before.

  Serv. Now I'll tell you without asking. My master is the great
    rich Capulet; and if you be not of the house of Montagues, I pray
    come and crush a cup of wine. Rest you merry! Exit.

  Ben. At this same ancient feast of Capulet's
    Sups the fair Rosaline whom thou so lov'st;
    With all the admired beauties of Verona.
    Go thither, and with unattainted eye
    Compare her face with some that I shall show,
    And I will make thee think thy swan a crow.

  Rom. When the devout religion of mine eye
    Maintains such falsehood, then turn tears to fires;
    And these, who, often drown'd, could never die,
    Transparent heretics, be burnt for liars!
    One fairer than my love? The all-seeing sun
    Ne'er saw her match since first the world begun.

Ben. Tut! you saw her fair, none else being by,
   Herself pois'd with herself in either eye;
   But in that crystal scales let there be weigh'd
   Your lady's love against some other maid
   That I will show you shining at this feast,
   And she shall scant show well that now seems best.

Rom. I'll go along, no such sight to be shown,
   But to rejoice in splendour of my own. [Exeunt.]

Summary

Paris Lord Capulet for authorization to wed Juliet, however Capulet demands that Paris ought to show restraint, since Juliet is just thirteen. In any case, Capulet grants Paris consent to charm Juliet and accordingly win her endorsement. Capulet proposes to Paris that he should attempt to dazzle Juliet at a conceal ball that the Capulets are facilitating that night. Capulet then hands his hireling Peter a rundown of names and requests the man to welcome everybody on the rundown to the gathering.

Out in the city, Peter runs into Romeo and Benvolio, who are discussing Rosaline. Dwindle can't peruse, so he requests that they assist him with interpretting the rundown. Romeo and Benvolio go along, and after perusing the rundown, they find that Rosaline will be at the Capulets' gathering. They choose to join in - despite the fact that it is a Capulet party, they will have the option to camouflage their personalities by wearing veils.

Scene III. Capulet's house.

Enter Capulet's Wife, and Nurse.

Wife. Nurse, where's my daughter? Call her forth to me.

Nurse. Now, by my maidenhead at twelve year old,
  I bade her come. What, lamb! what ladybird!
  God forbid! Where's this girl? What, Juliet!

Enter Juliet.

Jul. How now? Who calls?

Nurse. Your mother.

Jul. Madam, I am here.
  What is your will?

Wife. This is the matter- Nurse, give leave awhile,
  We must talk in secret. Nurse, come back again;
  I have rememb'red me, thou's hear our counsel.
  Thou knowest my daughter's of a pretty age.

Nurse. Faith, I can tell her age unto an hour.

Wife. She's not fourteen.

Nurse. I'll lay fourteen of my teeth-
  And yet, to my teen be it spoken, I have but four-

She is not fourteen. How long is it now
  To Lammastide?

Wife. A fortnight and odd days.

 Nurse. Even or odd, of all days in the year,
    Come Lammas Eve at night shall she be fourteen.
    Susan and she (God rest all Christian souls!)
    Were of an age. Well, Susan is with God;
    She was too good for me. But, as I said,
    On Lammas Eve at night shall she be fourteen;
    That shall she, marry; I remember it well.
    'Tis since the earthquake now eleven years;
    And she was wean'd (I never shall forget it),
    Of all the days of the year, upon that day;
    For I had then laid wormwood to my dug,
    Sitting in the sun under the dovehouse wall.
    My lord and you were then at Mantua.
    Nay, I do bear a brain. But, as I said,
    When it did taste the wormwood on the nipple
    Of my dug and felt it bitter, pretty fool,
    To see it tetchy and fall out with the dug!
    Shake, quoth the dovehouse! 'Twas no need, I trow,
    To bid me trudge.
    And since that time it is eleven years,
    For then she could stand high-lone; nay, by th' rood,
    She could have run and waddled all about;
    For even the day before, she broke her brow;
    And then my husband (God be with his soul!
    'A was a merry man) took up the child.
    'Yea,' quoth he, 'dost thou fall upon thy face?
    Thou wilt fall backward when thou hast more wit;
    Wilt thou not, Jule?' and, by my holidam,
    The pretty wretch left crying, and said 'Ay.'
    To see now how a jest shall come about!

I warrant, an I should live a thousand yeas,
I never should forget it. 'Wilt thou not, Jule?' quoth he,
And, pretty fool, it stinted, and said 'Ay.'

Wife. Enough of this. I pray thee hold thy peace.

Nurse. Yes, madam. Yet I cannot choose but laugh
To think it should leave crying and say 'Ay.'
And yet, I warrant, it bad upon it brow
A bump as big as a young cock'rel's stone;
A perilous knock; and it cried bitterly.
'Yea,' quoth my husband, 'fall'st upon thy face?
Thou wilt fall backward when thou comest to age;
Wilt thou not, Jule?' It stinted, and said 'Ay.'

Jul. And stint thou too, I pray thee, nurse, say I.

Nurse. Peace, I have done. God mark thee to his grace!
Thou wast the prettiest babe that e'er I nurs'd.
An I might live to see thee married once, I have my wish.

Wife. Marry, that 'marry' is the very theme
I came to talk of. Tell me, daughter Juliet,
How stands your disposition to be married?

Jul. It is an honour that I dream not of.

Nurse. An honour? Were not I thine only nurse,
I would say thou hadst suck'd wisdom from thy teat.

Wife. Well, think of marriage now. Younger than you,
Here in Verona, ladies of esteem,

Are made already mothers. By my count,
I was your mother much upon these years
That you are now a maid. Thus then in brief:
The valiant Paris seeks you for his love.

Nurse. A man, young lady! lady, such a man
As all the world- why he's a man of wax.

Wife. Verona's summer hath not such a flower.

Nurse. Nay, he's a flower, in faith- a very flower.

Wife. What say you? Can you love the gentleman?
This night you shall behold him at our feast.
Read o'er the volume of young Paris' face,
And find delight writ there with beauty's pen;
Examine every married lineament,
And see how one another lends content;
And what obscur'd in this fair volume lies
Find written in the margent of his eyes,
This precious book of love, this unbound lover,
To beautify him only lacks a cover.
The fish lives in the sea, and 'tis much pride
For fair without the fair within to hide.
That book in many's eyes doth share the glory,
That in gold clasps locks in the golden story;
So shall you share all that he doth possess,
By having him making yourself no less.

Nurse. No less? Nay, bigger! Women grow by men

Wife. Speak briefly, can you like of Paris' love?

Jul. I'll look to like, if looking liking move;
But no more deep will I endart mine eye

Than your consent gives strength to make it fly.

Enter Servingman.

Serv. Madam, the guests are come, supper serv'd up, you call'd, my young lady ask'd for, the nurse curs'd in the pantry, and everything in extremity. I must hence to wait. I beseech you follow straight.

   Wife. We follow thee. Exit [Servingman].
   Juliet, the County stays.

   Nurse. Go, girl, seek happy nights to happy days.
                         Exeunt.

Act One, Scene Three Summary

At the Capulet home, Lady Capulet approaches the Nurse to call for Juliet. While they anticipate the young lady's appearance, the Nurse mourns the way that Juliet will be fourteen in less than about fourteen days. When Juliet shows up, the Nurse tells a meandering aimlessly, humiliating anecdote about how her late spouse had once poked an unseemly sexual fun at Juliet when she was a newborn child. The Nurse continues disclosing to her unending story until Juliet orders her to stop.

Woman Capulet educates Juliet regarding Paris' aim to wed her. The mother depicts Paris as wonderful, contrasting him with a fine book that lone comes up short on a spread. Juliet doesn't guarantee anything to her mom, yet she agrees to contemplate Paris that night.

Scene IV. A street.

Enter Romeo, Mercutio, Benvolio, with five or six other Maskers;
Torchbearers.

Rom. What, shall this speech be spoke for our excuse?
  Or shall we on without apology?

Ben. The date is out of such prolixity.
  We'll have no Cupid hoodwink'd with a scarf,
  Bearing a Tartar's painted bow of lath,
  Scaring the ladies like a crowkeeper;
  Nor no without-book prologue, faintly spoke
  After the prompter, for our entrance;
  But, let them measure us by what they will,
  We'll measure them a measure, and be gone.

Rom. Give me a torch. I am not for this ambling.
  Being but heavy, I will bear the light.

Mer. Nay, gentle Romeo, we must have you dance.

Rom. Not I, believe me. You have dancing shoes
  With nimble soles; I have a soul of lead
  So stakes me to the ground I cannot move.

Mer. You are a lover. Borrow Cupid's wings
And soar with them above a common bound.

Rom. I am too sore enpierced with his shaft
To soar with his light feathers; and so bound
I cannot bound a pitch above dull woe.
Under love's heavy burthen do I sink.

Mer. And, to sink in it, should you burthen love-
Too great oppression for a tender thing.

Rom. Is love a tender thing? It is too rough,
Too rude, too boist'rous, and it pricks like thorn.

Mer. If love be rough with you, be rough with love.
Prick love for pricking, and you beat love down.
Give me a case to put my visage in.
A visor for a visor! What care I
What curious eye doth quote deformities?
Here are the beetle brows shall blush for me.

Ben. Come, knock and enter; and no sooner in
But every man betake him to his legs.

Rom. A torch for me! Let wantons light of heart
Tickle the senseless rushes with their heels;
For I am proverb'd with a grandsire phrase,
I'll be a candle-holder and look on;
The game was ne'er so fair, and I am done.

Mer. Tut! dun's the mouse, the constable's own word!
If thou art Dun, we'll draw thee from the mire
Of this sir-reverence love, wherein thou stick'st
Up to the ears. Come, we burn daylight, ho!

Rom. Nay, that's not so.

Mer. I mean, sir, in delay
We waste our lights in vain, like lamps by day.
Take our good meaning, for our judgment sits
Five times in that ere once in our five wits.

Rom. And we mean well, in going to this masque;
But 'tis no wit to go.

Mer. Why, may one ask?

Rom. I dreamt a dream to-night.

Mer. And so did I.

Rom. Well, what was yours?

Mer. That dreamers often lie.

Rom. In bed asleep, while they do dream things true.

Mer. O, then I see Queen Mab hath been with you.
She is the fairies' midwife, and she comes
In shape no bigger than an agate stone
On the forefinger of an alderman,
Drawn with a team of little atomies
Athwart men's noses as they lie asleep;
Her wagon spokes made of long spinners' legs,
The cover, of the wings of grasshoppers;
Her traces, of the smallest spider's web;

Her collars, of the moonshine's wat'ry beams;
Her whip, of cricket's bone; the lash, of film;
Her wagoner, a small grey-coated gnat,
Not half so big as a round little worm
Prick'd from the lazy finger of a maid;
Her chariot is an empty hazelnut,
Made by the joiner squirrel or old grub,
Time out o' mind the fairies' coachmakers.
And in this state she 'gallops night by night
Through lovers' brains, and then they dream of love;
O'er courtiers' knees, that dream on cursies straight;
O'er lawyers' fingers, who straight dream on fees;
O'er ladies' lips, who straight on kisses dream,
Which oft the angry Mab with blisters plagues,
Because their breaths with sweetmeats tainted are.
Sometime she gallops o'er a courtier's nose,
And then dreams he of smelling out a suit;
And sometime comes she with a tithe-pig's tail
Tickling a parson's nose as 'a lies asleep,
Then dreams he of another benefice.
Sometimes she driveth o'er a soldier's neck,
And then dreams he of cutting foreign throats,
Of breaches, ambuscadoes, Spanish blades,
Of healths five fadom deep; and then anon
Drums in his ear, at which he starts and wakes,
And being thus frighted, swears a prayer or two
And sleeps again. This is that very Mab
That plats the manes of horses in the night
And bakes the elflocks in foul sluttish, hairs,
Which once untangled much misfortune bodes
This is the hag, when maids lie on their backs,
That presses them and learns them first to bear,
Making them women of good carriage.
This is she-

Rom. Peace, peace, Mercutio, peace!
　Thou talk'st of nothing.

Mer. True, I talk of dreams;
　Which are the children of an idle brain,
　Begot of nothing but vain fantasy;
　Which is as thin of substance as the air,
　And more inconstant than the wind, who wooes
　Even now the frozen bosom of the North
　And, being anger'd, puffs away from thence,
　Turning his face to the dew-dropping South.

Ben. This wind you talk of blows us from ourselves.
　Supper is done, and we shall come too late.

Rom. I fear, too early; for my mind misgives
　Some consequence, yet hanging in the stars,
　Shall bitterly begin his fearful date
　With this night's revels and expire the term
　Of a despised life, clos'd in my breast,
　By some vile forfeit of untimely death.
　But he that hath the steerage of my course
　Direct my sail! On, lusty gentlemen!

Ben. Strike, drum.
　　　　　They march about the stage. [Exeunt.]

Act One, Scene Four Summary

Romeo, Benvolio, and their companion Mercutio stroll through the boulevards to the Capulets' gathering. Romeo stays discouraged over Rosaline, so Mercutio attempts to brighten him up with a tale about Queen Mab, an invented mythical person who penetrates men's fantasies. Romeo quiets his companion, conceding his anxiety about the going to a gathering at the home of his adversaries.

Scene V. Capulet's house.

Servingmen come forth with napkins.

   1. Serv. Where's Potpan, that he helps not to take away?
     He shift a trencher! he scrape a trencher!
   2. Serv. When good manners shall lie all in one or two men's
     hands, and they unwash'd too, 'tis a foul thing.
   1. Serv. Away with the join-stools, remove the court-cubbert,
     look to the plate. Good thou, save me a piece of marchpane and, as
     thou loves me, let the porter let in Susan Grindstone and
Nell.
     Anthony, and Potpan!
   2. Serv. Ay, boy, ready.
   1. Serv. You are look'd for and call'd for, ask'd for and
     sought for, in the great chamber.
   3. Serv. We cannot be here and there too. Cheerly, boys!

Be brisk awhile, and the longer liver take all. *Exeunt.*

Enter the Maskers, Enter, [with Servants,] Capulet, his Wife,
      Juliet, Tybalt, and all the Guests
        and Gentlewomen to the Maskers.

 Cap. Welcome, gentlemen! Ladies that have their toes
  Unplagu'd with corns will have a bout with you.
  Ah ha, my mistresses! which of you all
  Will now deny to dance? She that makes dainty,
  She I'll swear hath corns. Am I come near ye now?
  Welcome, gentlemen! I have seen the day
  That I have worn a visor and could tell
  A whispering tale in a fair lady's ear,
  Such as would please. 'Tis gone, 'tis gone, 'tis gone!
  You are welcome, gentlemen! Come, musicians, play.
  A hall, a hall! give room! and foot it, girls.
              Music plays, and they dance.
  More light, you knaves! and turn the tables up,
  And quench the fire, the room is grown too hot.
  Ah, sirrah, this unlook'd-for sport comes well.
  Nay, sit, nay, sit, good cousin Capulet,
  For you and I are past our dancing days.
  How long is't now since last yourself and I
  Were in a mask?
 2. Cap. By'r Lady, thirty years.

 Cap. What, man? 'Tis not so much, 'tis not so much!
  'Tis since the nuptial of Lucentio,
  Come Pentecost as quickly as it will,
  Some five-and-twenty years, and then we mask'd.
 2. Cap. 'Tis more, 'tis more! His son is elder, sir;

His son is thirty.

Cap. Will you tell me that?
His son was but a ward two years ago.

Rom. [to a Servingman] What lady's that, which doth enrich the
   hand Of yonder knight?

Serv. I know not, sir.

Rom. O, she doth teach the torches to burn bright!
It seems she hangs upon the cheek of night
Like a rich jewel in an Ethiop's ear-
Beauty too rich for use, for earth too dear!
So shows a snowy dove trooping with crows
As yonder lady o'er her fellows shows.
The measure done, I'll watch her place of stand
And, touching hers, make blessed my rude hand.
Did my heart love till now? Forswear it, sight!
For I ne'er saw true beauty till this night.

Tyb. This, by his voice, should be a Montague.
Fetch me my rapier, boy. What, dares the slave
Come hither, cover'd with an antic face,
To fleer and scorn at our solemnity?
Now, by the stock and honour of my kin,
To strike him dead I hold it not a sin.

Cap. Why, how now, kinsman? Wherefore storm you so?

Tyb. Uncle, this is a Montague, our foe;
A villain, that is hither come in spite

To scorn at our solemnity this night.

Cap. Young Romeo is it?

Tyb. 'Tis he, that villain Romeo.

Cap. Content thee, gentle coz, let him alone.
'A bears him like a portly gentleman,
And, to say truth, Verona brags of him
To be a virtuous and well-govern'd youth.
I would not for the wealth of all this town
Here in my house do him disparagement.
Therefore be patient, take no note of him.
It is my will; the which if thou respect,
Show a fair presence and put off these frowns,
An ill-beseeming semblance for a feast.

Tyb. It fits when such a villain is a guest.
I'll not endure him.

Cap. He shall be endur'd.
What, goodman boy? I say he shall. Go to!
Am I the master here, or you? Go to!
You'll not endure him? God shall mend my soul!
You'll make a mutiny among my guests!
You will set cock-a-hoop! you'll be the man!

Tyb. Why, uncle, 'tis a shame.

Cap. Go to, go to!
You are a saucy boy. Is't so, indeed?
This trick may chance to scathe you. I know what.
You must contrary me! Marry, 'tis time.-
Well said, my hearts!- You are a princox- go!

Be quiet, or- More light, more light!- For shame!
I'll make you quiet; what!- Cheerly, my hearts!

Tyb. Patience perforce with wilful choler meeting
Makes my flesh tremble in their different greeting.
I will withdraw; but this intrusion shall,
Now seeming sweet, convert to bitt'rest gall. Exit.

Rom. If I profane with my unworthiest hand
This holy shrine, the gentle fine is this:
My lips, two blushing pilgrims, ready stand
To smooth that rough touch with a tender kiss.

Jul. Good pilgrim, you do wrong your hand too much,
Which mannerly devotion shows in this;
For saints have hands that pilgrims' hands do touch,
And palm to palm is holy palmers' kiss.

Rom. Have not saints lips, and holy palmers too?

Jul. Ay, pilgrim, lips that they must use in pray'r.

Rom. O, then, dear saint, let lips do what hands do!
They pray; grant thou, lest faith turn to despair.

Jul. Saints do not move, though grant for prayers' sake.

Rom. Then move not while my prayer's effect I take.
Thus from my lips, by thine my sin is purg'd. [Kisses her.]

Jul. Then have my lips the sin that they have took.

Rom. Sin from my lips? O trespass sweetly urg'd!
Give me my sin again. [Kisses her.]

Jul. You kiss by th' book.

Nurse. Madam, your mother craves a word with you.

Rom. What is her mother?

Nurse. Marry, bachelor,
Her mother is the lady of the house.
And a good lady, and a wise and virtuous.
I nurs'd her daughter that you talk'd withal.
I tell you, he that can lay hold of her
Shall have the chinks.

Rom. Is she a Capulet?
O dear account! my life is my foe's debt.

Ben. Away, be gone; the sport is at the best.

Rom. Ay, so I fear; the more is my unrest.

Cap. Nay, gentlemen, prepare not to be gone;
We have a trifling foolish banquet towards.
Is it e'en so? Why then, I thank you all.
I thank you, honest gentlemen. Good night.
More torches here! [Exeunt Maskers.] Come on then, let's to bed.
Ah, sirrah, by my fay, it waxes late;
I'll to my rest.
                Exeunt [all but Juliet and Nurse].

Jul. Come hither, nurse. What is yond gentleman?

Nurse. The son and heir of old Tiberio.

Jul. What's he that now is going out of door?

Nurse. Marry, that, I think, be young Petruchio.

Jul. What's he that follows there, that would not dance?

Nurse. I know not.

Jul. Go ask his name.- If he be married,
My grave is like to be my wedding bed.

Nurse. His name is Romeo, and a Montague,
The only son of your great enemy.

Jul. My only love, sprung from my only hate!
Too early seen unknown, and known too late!
Prodigious birth of love it is to me
That I must love a loathed enemy.

Nurse. What's this? what's this?

Jul. A rhyme I learnt even now
Of one I danc'd withal.
                  One calls within, 'Juliet.'

Nurse. Anon, anon!
Come, let's away; the strangers all are gone. Exeunt.

Act One, Scene Five Summary

At the gathering, Romeo sulks in the corner, away from the moving. From this vantage point, he sees Juliet, and begins to look all starry eyed at her right away.

Tybalt catches Romeo getting some information about Juliet, and perceives the conceal man's voice. In any case, before Tybalt can make a scene, Lord Capulet helps him to remember the sovereign's preclusion of open battling, and requests the kid to remain down.

Romeo approaches Juliet and contacts her hand. They talk together in a piece, and Romeo inevitably acquires Juliet's consent for a kiss. Be that as it may, before they can talk further, the Nurse calls Juliet to see her mom. After Juliet leaves, Romeo asks the Nurse her name, and is stunned to discover that his new object of want is a Capulet.

As the gathering slows down, Juliet gets some information about Romeo. At the point when she finds out about Romeo's personality, she is shattered to discover that she has begun to look all starry eyed at a "hated foe" (1.5.138).

Act 1 Analysis

Despite the fact that Romeo and Juliet is apparently a catastrophe, it has suffered as one of Shakespeare's most prestigious perfect works of art as a result of its radiant mix of styles and amazing, multi-faceted character advancement. The play frequently veers from fastidious plot into all the more freestyle investigations, making it hard to sort. In any case, these are uniquely Shakespearean characteristics that are evident from the play's first Act. Romeo and Juliet starts with a Chorus, which builds up the plot and tone of the play. This gadget was not really new to Shakespeare, and in actuality reflects the structure of Arthur Brooke's The Tragical History of Romeus and Juliet, from which Shakespeare adjusted Romeo and Juliet.

Furthermore, the Chorus suggests the conversation starter of whether Romeo and Juliet is a disaster. During Shakespeare's time, it was average for a disaster in the first place a Chorus. In Romeo and Juliet, the initial poem presents critical enough conditions to help that show. In any case, catastrophe in its strictest structure assumes certain conventional arrogances. Most significant is the possibility that an individual (or people) is (or are) vanquished by powers past their control; catastrophes regularly commend human self control despite misfortune or awesome threat. But then, the powers at play in Romeo and Juliet are barely outside human ability to control. Rather, the Montagues and Capulets have permitted their quarrel to rot. This is obvious from the main scene, when even the patriarchs of the two families enter the open road battle, prepared to execute. The Chorus acquaints Shakespeare's exceptional methodology with disaster by presenting certain built up tropes of that type however by declining to lay the fault at the universe's feet.

What's more, the Chorus additionally presents certain wellsprings of emotional pressure that re-show up all through the remainder of the play. For instance, the polar restriction among request and confusion is fundamental to Romeo and Juliet. In the Prologue, the Chorus talks in poem structure, which was normally saved for a darling tending to his dearest. The work is an extremely organized type of verse, which shows a degree of request. Nonetheless, the substance of this poem – two families who can't control themselves, and subsequently cut down fiasco on their heads – proposes mind boggling jumble. The contention among request and turmoil resounds through the remainder of Act I. Promptly following the Sonnet is the presentation of Sampson and Gregory, two brutish men whose appearance lays the preparation for a disarranged road fight. Besides, the turmoil inside the play is confirm by reversed conditions. Workers start the fight, however before long draw the aristocrats into it. The youngsters enter the battle, however the more established men before long attempt to resist their matured bodies by taking an interest. Besides, the way that the close to calamity happens without trying to hide in an open spot undermines any desire for security in Verona.

This fundamental topic of turmoil is additionally show in the cross breed of styles that Shakespeare utilizes. The Chorus sets up the way that the story is intended to be deplorable, but then, Abram and Gregory are normally funny characters, both in light of their low status and the carefree idea of their discourse. While they do examine their hostility towards the Capulets, they likewise make various sexual plays on words, without a doubt planned to entertain the crowd. That these sexual insinuations regularly slide into brutal discuss assault just underscores the trouble of sorting Shakespeare's tonal expectations.

Note that Shakespeare needed Romeo and Juliet to be perceived as disaster, despite the fact that he subverts the class from multiple points of view. There are a couple of themes in Romeo and Juliet that uncover this expectation. The first is the common theme of death. In Act I, there are a few minutes where the characters foretell the demise to come. After she meets Romeo, Juliet states, "On the off chance that he be hitched,/My grave resembles to be my wedding bed" (1.5.132). When Benvolio attempts to stop the road battle, he comments, "Set up your swords. You know not what you do" (1.1.56). The expressing of Benvolio's line is a Biblical reference since it brings out Jesus' request that his witnesses stop battling the Roman gatekeepers during his capture. This imagery hints Juliet's passing, which happens after her restoration.

The Nurse likewise makes two references that portend Juliet's passing. In the story she advises to Lady Capulet, the Nurse discusses Juliet's fall when she was a youngster. The story anticipates the way that Juilet will fall, bringing out the medieval and Renaissance idea of the wheel of fortune. Through the span of the play, Juliet without a doubt rises (showing up at her overhang to address Romeo) and falls (her passing in the vault). The Nurse additionally foretells the disaster when she tells Juliet, "An I may live to see thee wedded once" (1.3.63). Tsk-tsk, this is actually what will happen, and Juliet bites the dust scarcely one day after her marriage. So even as he veers among styles and structures, Shakespeare ensures that Romeo and Juliet a terrible story.

Significantly more great than his elaborate virtuosity is Shakespeare's painstakingly adjusted character advancement. Pretty much every character in Romeo and Juliet uncovers their internal nature through activity. For example, we learn in Act 1 that Benvolio is a radical, while Tybalt is hot-headed. Different characters that Shakespeare presents in Act 1 uncover a gleam of their internal wants regardless of whether they don't yet get an opportunity to communicate them. For example, in the scene between Lord Capulet and Paris, the patriarch acquaints his longing with control his little girl. While hypothetically safeguarding Juliet's young opportunity, he additionally uncovers his propensity to think about her as an article by conceding Paris the chance to charm her. Ruler Capulet's mentality towards Juliet will later power the last, heartbreaking new development.

Prominent abstract pundit Harold Bloom accepts that, alongside Juliet, Mercutio and the Nurse are Shakespeare's most sublime manifestations in the play. The Nurse is charming a direct result of her self-double dealing. While she professes to think about youthful Juliet, it becomes obvious that she egotistically wishes to control the young lady. Her anecdote about Juliet's fall and sharing her late spouse's sexual joke are fiercely unseemly remarks, and uncover the Nurse's self-fixation and her interest with sex. For such an utilitarian character, the Nurse is especially significant, and a brilliant illustration of Shakespeare's capacity to make multi-faceted characters, in any event, for his supporting characters.

Thus, Shakespeare uncovers a ton about Mercutio's character in the youngster's Queen Mab discourse. From the outset, the discourse (and the previous scene) paint Mercutio as a brilliant, explicitly disapproved of individual, who favors transient yearn for submitted love. Nonetheless, as his discourse proceeds, Mercutio depicts a degree of force that Romeo needs. Sovereign Mab is a somewhat horrible figure who powers sexuality upon ladies in a to a great extent unsavory and brutal way. While he shares this story, Mercutio's tone turns out to be energetic to the point that Romeo should commandingly quieten him. This discourse fills in as a sign that Mercutio is a definitely more full grown and savvy figure than his conduct quickly proposes.

Interestingly, Prince Escalus and the Citizens of the Watch are to a great extent two-dimensional characters. They fill a simply utilitarian need, speaking to peace in Verona. While the Prince habitually shows solid position - announcing road battling unlawful and later, banishing Romeo - his declarations just produce insignificant outcomes, and the law is never as incredible as the powers of affection in the play. Then, the Citizens of the Watch, however quiet, are a gesture to the general public's endeavors to secure itself. Shakespeare routinely shows that the Citizens are in every case close by, which accentuates the continuous clash between the fighting families and society's endeavors to reestablish request.

Despite the fact that Romeo and Juliet has become a prototype romantic tale, it is in reality an impression of just a single unmistakable kind of adoration – a youthful, nonsensical love that falls somewhere close to unadulterated friendship and unbridled desire. Sexuality is widespread all through the play, beginning with the hirelings' risqué jokes in the principal scene. Likewise, the sweethearts don't think about their enthusiasm in strict terms (a strict association would have meant an unadulterated love to a Renaissance crowd)

In the mean time, Romeo is a far less intricate character than Juliet – undoubtedly, in Shakespeare's work, the courageous women are regularly more multi-dimensional than their male partners. In Act 1, Romeo's most articulated characteristics are his peevishness and inclination. His companions (and possibly, the crowd) see Romeo's despairing mind-set as grinding, and are confounded when he rapidly overlooks Rosaline to fall frantically enamored with Juliet. In any case, Romeo stands separated from different men in Act 1. Indeed, even Benvolio, the unceasing conservative, has perceived the brutal idea of the world, and the majority of different men rapidly go to outrage and hostility as answers for their issues. Romeo, then again, shows characteristics that could be viewed as ladylike by Shakespearean guidelines – he is despairing and withdrawn, deciding to stay far off from both the quarrel and the brutality in Verona.

Juliet, then again, is thoughtful and down to earth. At the point when her mom demands she think about Paris as a potential mate, Juliet is obviously uninterested, yet comprehends that a vocal refusal will pick up her nothing. Her demonstration of blameless accommodation will permit her to be insidious later on, to her favorable position. In Act 1, Juliet is now giving her forces of double dealing by getting some information about two other men before asking after Romeo since she wouldn't like to stimulate her chaperone's doubts.

PROLOGUE

Enter Chorus.

  Chor. Now old desire doth in his deathbed lie,
    And young affection gapes to be his heir;
    That fair for which love groan'd for and would die,
    With tender Juliet match'd, is now not fair.
    Now Romeo is belov'd, and loves again,
    Alike bewitched by the charm of looks;
    But to his foe suppos'd he must complain,
    And she steal love's sweet bait from fearful hooks.
    Being held a foe, he may not have access
    To breathe such vows as lovers use to swear,
    And she as much in love, her means much less
    To meet her new beloved anywhere;
    But passion lends them power, time means, to meet,
    Temp'ring extremities with extreme sweet.
Exit.

ACT II. Scene I. A lane by the wall of Capulet's orchard.

Enter Romeo alone.

  Rom. Can I go forward when my heart is here?
    Turn back, dull earth, and find thy centre out.
        [Climbs the wall and leaps down within it.]

Enter Benvolio with Mercutio.

Ben. Romeo! my cousin Romeo! Romeo!

Mer. He is wise,
And, on my life, hath stol'n him home to bed.

Ben. He ran this way, and leapt this orchard wall.
Call, good Mercutio.

Mer. Nay, I'll conjure too.
Romeo! humours! madman! passion! lover!
Appear thou in the likeness of a sigh;
Speak but one rhyme, and I am satisfied!
Cry but 'Ay me!' pronounce but 'love' and 'dove';
Speak to my gossip Venus one fair word,
One nickname for her purblind son and heir,
Young Adam Cupid, he that shot so trim
When King Cophetua lov'd the beggar maid!
He heareth not, he stirreth not, be moveth not;
The ape is dead, and I must conjure him.
I conjure thee by Rosaline's bright eyes.
By her high forehead and her scarlet lip,
By her fine foot, straight leg, and quivering thigh,
And the demesnes that there adjacent lie,
That in thy likeness thou appear to us!

Ben. An if he hear thee, thou wilt anger him.

Mer. This cannot anger him. 'Twould anger him
To raise a spirit in his mistress' circle
Of some strange nature, letting it there stand
Till she had laid it and conjur'd it down.
That were some spite; my invocation
Is fair and honest: in his mistress' name,
I conjure only but to raise up him.

Ben. Come, he hath hid himself among these trees
To be consorted with the humorous night.
Blind is his love and best befits the dark.

Mer. If love be blind, love cannot hit the mark.
Now will he sit under a medlar tree
And wish his mistress were that kind of fruit
As maids call medlars when they laugh alone.
O, Romeo, that she were, O that she were
An open et cetera, thou a pop'rin pear!
Romeo, good night. I'll to my truckle-bed;
This field-bed is too cold for me to sleep.
Come, shall we go?

Ben. Go then, for 'tis in vain
'To seek him here that means not to be found.
                             Exeunt.

Act Two, Scene One Summary

Out in the road, Romeo escapes from Mercutio and Benvolio. Mercutio calls to him, utilizing loads of vulgar wit. Benvolio at last becomes weary of scanning for Romeo, and they leave.

(It would be ideal if you note that a few versions of Romeo and Juliet end Scene One here to start another one. Others, including the Norton Shakespeare, which this note depends on, proceed with the scene as follows.)
In the interim, Romeo has prevailing with regards to jumping over the Capulets' nursery divider and is stowing away underneath Juliet's overhang. He needs to decide if her fascination is equivalent to his own. She

before long shows up and conveys her celebrated talk, asking "Goodness Romeo, Romeo, wherefore workmanship thou Romeo?" (2.1.75). She wishes that Romeo's name were extraordinary, with the goal that they would not be foes. Romeo catches her discourse, which affirms his own emotions. He intrudes on Juliet to admit his own affection.

Juliet cautions Romeo to talk honestly, since she has begun to look all starry eyed at him and wouldn't like to be harmed. Romeo swears his emotions are certified, and Juliet regrets the way that she can't go gaga for him once more. The Nurse calls to Juliet, who vanishes quickly. She returns out and demands that if Romeo really cherishes her, he ought to propose marriage and plan a gathering place for them. The Nurse calls Juliet a subsequent time, and she exits. Romeo is going to leave when his affection develops yet a third time, and gets back to him for some last expressions of separating.

Scene II. Capulet's orchard.

Enter Romeo.

Rom. He jests at scars that never felt a wound.

Enter Juliet above at a window.

> But soft! What light through yonder window breaks?
> It is the East, and Juliet is the sun!
> Arise, fair sun, and kill the envious moon,
> Who is already sick and pale with grief
> That thou her maid art far more fair than she.
> Be not her maid, since she is envious.
> Her vestal livery is but sick and green,
> And none but fools do wear it. Cast it off.
> It is my lady; O, it is my love!

O that she knew she were!
She speaks, yet she says nothing. What of that?
Her eye discourses; I will answer it.
I am too bold; 'tis not to me she speaks.
Two of the fairest stars in all the heaven,
Having some business, do entreat her eyes
To twinkle in their spheres till they return.
What if her eyes were there, they in her head?
The brightness of her cheek would shame those stars
As daylight doth a lamp; her eyes in heaven
Would through the airy region stream so bright
That birds would sing and think it were not night.
See how she leans her cheek upon her hand!
O that I were a glove upon that hand,
That I might touch that cheek!

Jul. Ay me!

Rom. She speaks.
O, speak again, bright angel! for thou art
As glorious to this night, being o'er my head,
As is a winged messenger of heaven
Unto the white-upturned wond'ring eyes
Of mortals that fall back to gaze on him
When he bestrides the lazy-pacing clouds
And sails upon the bosom of the air.

Jul. O Romeo, Romeo! wherefore art thou Romeo?
Deny thy father and refuse thy name!
Or, if thou wilt not, be but sworn my love,
And I'll no longer be a Capulet.

Rom. [aside] Shall I hear more, or shall I speak at this?

Jul. 'Tis but thy name that is my enemy.
Thou art thyself, though not a Montague.
What's Montague? it is nor hand, nor foot,
Nor arm, nor face, nor any other part
Belonging to a man. O, be some other name!
What's in a name? That which we call a rose
By any other name would smell as sweet.
So Romeo would, were he not Romeo call'd,
Retain that dear perfection which he owes
Without that title. Romeo, doff thy name;
And for that name, which is no part of thee,
Take all myself.

Rom. I take thee at thy word.
Call me but love, and I'll be new baptiz'd;
Henceforth I never will be Romeo.

Jul. What man art thou that, thus bescreen'd in night,
So stumblest on my counsel?

Rom. By a name
I know not how to tell thee who I am.
My name, dear saint, is hateful to myself,
Because it is an enemy to thee.
Had I it written, I would tear the word.

Jul. My ears have yet not drunk a hundred words
Of that tongue's utterance, yet I know the sound.
Art thou not Romeo, and a Montague?

Rom. Neither, fair saint, if either thee dislike.

Jul. How cam'st thou hither, tell me, and wherefore?
  The orchard walls are high and hard to climb,
  And the place death, considering who thou art,
  If any of my kinsmen find thee here.

  Rom. With love's light wings did I o'erperch these walls;
    For stony limits cannot hold love out,
    And what love can do, that dares love attempt.
    Therefore thy kinsmen are no let to me.

Jul. If they do see thee, they will murther thee.

  Rom. Alack, there lies more peril in thine eye
    Than twenty of their swords! Look thou but sweet,
    And I am proof against their enmity.

Jul. I would not for the world they saw thee here.

  Rom. I have night's cloak to hide me from their sight;
    And but thou love me, let them find me here.
    My life were better ended by their hate
    Than death prorogued, wanting of thy love.

Jul. By whose direction found'st thou out this place?

  Rom. By love, that first did prompt me to enquire.
    He lent me counsel, and I lent him eyes.
    I am no pilot; yet, wert thou as far
    As that vast shore wash'd with the farthest sea,
    I would adventure for such merchandise.

Jul. Thou knowest the mask of night is on my face;
Else would a maiden blush bepaint my cheek
For that which thou hast heard me speak to-night.
Fain would I dwell on form- fain, fain deny
What I have spoke; but farewell compliment!
Dost thou love me, I know thou wilt say 'Ay';
And I will take thy word. Yet, if thou swear'st,
Thou mayst prove false. At lovers' perjuries,
They say Jove laughs. O gentle Romeo,
If thou dost love, pronounce it faithfully.
Or if thou thinkest I am too quickly won,
I'll frown, and be perverse, and say thee nay,
So thou wilt woo; but else, not for the world.
In truth, fair Montague, I am too fond,
And therefore thou mayst think my haviour light;
But trust me, gentleman, I'll prove more true
Than those that have more cunning to be strange.
I should have been more strange, I must confess,
But that thou overheard'st, ere I was ware,
My true-love passion. Therefore pardon me,
And not impute this yielding to light love,
Which the dark night hath so discovered.

Rom. Lady, by yonder blessed moon I swear,
That tips with silver all these fruit-tree tops-

Jul. O, swear not by the moon, th' inconstant moon,
That monthly changes in her circled orb,
Lest that thy love prove likewise variable.

Rom. What shall I swear by?

Jul. Do not swear at all;
Or if thou wilt, swear by thy gracious self,

Which is the god of my idolatry,
And I'll believe thee.

Rom. If my heart's dear love—

Jul. Well, do not swear. Although I joy in thee,
I have no joy of this contract to-night.
It is too rash, too unadvis'd, too sudden;
Too like the lightning, which doth cease to be
Ere one can say 'It lightens.' Sweet, good night!
This bud of love, by summer's ripening breath,
May prove a beauteous flow'r when next we meet.
Good night, good night! As sweet repose and rest
Come to thy heart as that within my breast!

Rom. O, wilt thou leave me so unsatisfied?

Jul. What satisfaction canst thou have to-night?

Rom. Th' exchange of thy love's faithful vow for mine.

Jul. I gave thee mine before thou didst request it;
And yet I would it were to give again.

Rom. Would'st thou withdraw it? For what purpose, love?

Jul. But to be frank and give it thee again.
And yet I wish but for the thing I have.
My bounty is as boundless as the sea,
My love as deep; the more I give to thee,
The more I have, for both are infinite.
I hear some noise within. Dear love, adieu!
                    [Nurse] calls within.
Anon, good nurse! Sweet Montague, be true.

Stay but a little, I will come again. [Exit.]

Rom. O blessed, blessed night! I am afeard,
Being in night, all this is but a dream,
Too flattering-sweet to be substantial.

Enter Juliet above.

Jul. Three words, dear Romeo, and good night indeed.
If that thy bent of love be honourable,
Thy purpose marriage, send me word to-morrow,
By one that I'll procure to come to thee,
Where and what time thou wilt perform the rite;
And all my fortunes at thy foot I'll lay
And follow thee my lord throughout the world.

Nurse. (within) Madam!

Jul. I come, anon.- But if thou meanest not well,
I do beseech thee-

Nurse. (within) Madam!

Jul. By-and-by I come.-
To cease thy suit and leave me to my grief.
To-morrow will I send.

Rom. So thrive my soul-

Jul. A thousand times good night! Exit.

Rom. A thousand times the worse, to want thy light!
Love goes toward love as schoolboys from their books;

But love from love, towards school with heavy looks.

Enter Juliet again, [above].

Jul. Hist! Romeo, hist! O for a falconer's voice
To lure this tassel-gentle back again!
Bondage is hoarse and may not speak aloud;
Else would I tear the cave where Echo lies,
And make her airy tongue more hoarse than mine
With repetition of my Romeo's name.
Romeo!

Rom. It is my soul that calls upon my name.
How silver-sweet sound lovers' tongues by night,
Like softest music to attending ears!

Jul. Romeo!

Rom. My dear?

Jul. At what o'clock to-morrow
Shall I send to thee?

Rom. By the hour of nine.

Jul. I will not fail. 'Tis twenty years till then.
I have forgot why I did call thee back.

Rom. Let me stand here till thou remember it.

Jul. I shall forget, to have thee still stand there,
Rememb'ring how I love thy company.

Rom. And I'll still stay, to have thee still forget,
Forgetting any other home but this.

Jul. 'Tis almost morning. I would have thee gone-
And yet no farther than a wanton's bird,
That lets it hop a little from her hand,
Like a poor prisoner in his twisted gyves,
And with a silk thread plucks it back again,
So loving-jealous of his liberty.

Rom. I would I were thy bird.

Jul. Sweet, so would I.
Yet I should kill thee with much cherishing.
Good night, good night! Parting is such sweet sorrow,
That I shall say good night till it be morrow.
[Exit.]

Rom. Sleep dwell upon thine eyes, peace in thy breast!
Would I were sleep and peace, so sweet to rest!
Hence will I to my ghostly father's cell,
His help to crave and my dear hap to tell.
Exit

Act Two, Scene Two Summary

At the house of prayer, Friar Laurence is gathering herbs. Romeo shows up and admits his new love for Juliet. He requests that the Friar wed them. Despite the fact that the Friar is amazed that Romeo has overlooked Rosaline so rapidly, he is in any case charmed, in light of the fact that Romeo and Juliet's association presents a chance to control the furious quarrel between the Montagues and Capulets.

Scene III. Friar Laurence's cell.

Enter Friar, [Laurence] alone, with a basket.

  Friar. The grey-ey'd morn smiles on the frowning night,
    Check'ring the Eastern clouds with streaks of light;
    And flecked darkness like a drunkard reels
    From forth day's path and Titan's fiery wheels.
    Non, ere the sun advance his burning eye
    The day to cheer and night's dank dew to dry,
    I must up-fill this osier cage of ours
    With baleful weeds and precious-juiced flowers.
    The earth that's nature's mother is her tomb.
    What is her burying gave, that is her womb;
    And from her womb children of divers kind
    We sucking on her natural bosom find;
    Many for many virtues excellent,
    None but for some, and yet all different.
    O, mickle is the powerful grace that lies
    In plants, herbs, stones, and their true qualities;
    For naught so vile that on the earth doth live
    But to the earth some special good doth give;
    Nor aught so good but, strain'd from that fair use,

Revolts from true birth, stumbling on abuse.
Virtue itself turns vice, being misapplied,
And vice sometime's by action dignified.
Within the infant rind of this small flower
Poison hath residence, and medicine power;
For this, being smelt, with that part cheers each part;
Being tasted, slays all senses with the heart.
Two such opposed kings encamp them still
In man as well as herbs- grace and rude will;
And where the worser is predominant,
Full soon the canker death eats up that plant.

Enter Romeo.

Rom. Good morrow, father.

Friar. Benedicite!
What early tongue so sweet saluteth me?
Young son, it argues a distempered head
So soon to bid good morrow to thy bed.
Care keeps his watch in every old man's eye,
And where care lodges sleep will never lie;
But where unbruised youth with unstuff'd brain
Doth couch his limbs, there golden sleep doth reign.
Therefore thy earliness doth me assure
Thou art uprous'd with some distemp'rature;
Or if not so, then here I hit it right-
Our Romeo hath not been in bed to-night.

Rom. That last is true-the sweeter rest was mine.

Friar. God pardon sin! Wast thou with Rosaline?

Rom. With Rosaline, my ghostly father? No.
I have forgot that name, and that name's woe.

Friar. That's my good son! But where hast thou been then?

Rom. I'll tell thee ere thou ask it me again.
I have been feasting with mine enemy,
Where on a sudden one hath wounded me
That's by me wounded. Both our remedies
Within thy help and holy physic lies.
I bear no hatred, blessed man, for, lo,
My intercession likewise steads my foe.

Friar. Be plain, good son, and homely in thy drift
Riddling confession finds but riddling shrift.

Rom. Then plainly know my heart's dear love is set
On the fair daughter of rich Capulet;
As mine on hers, so hers is set on mine,
And all combin'd, save what thou must combine
By holy marriage. When, and where, and how
We met, we woo'd, and made exchange of vow,
I'll tell thee as we pass; but this I pray,
That thou consent to marry us to-day.

Friar. Holy Saint Francis! What a change is here!
Is Rosaline, that thou didst love so dear,
So soon forsaken? Young men's love then lies
Not truly in their hearts, but in their eyes.
Jesu Maria! What a deal of brine
Hath wash'd thy sallow cheeks for Rosaline!
How much salt water thrown away in waste,

To season love, that of it doth not taste!
The sun not yet thy sighs from heaven clears,
Thy old groans ring yet in mine ancient ears.
Lo, here upon thy cheek the stain doth sit
Of an old tear that is not wash'd off yet.
If e'er thou wast thyself, and these woes thine,
Thou and these woes were all for Rosaline.
And art thou chang'd? Pronounce this sentence then:
Women may fall when there's no strength in men.

Rom. Thou chid'st me oft for loving Rosaline.

Friar. For doting, not for loving, pupil mine.

Rom. And bad'st me bury love.

  Friar. Not in a grave
    To lay one in, another out to have.

  Rom. I pray thee chide not. She whom I love now
    Doth grace for grace and love for love allow.
    The other did not so.

  Friar. O, she knew well
    Thy love did read by rote, that could not spell.
    But come, young waverer, come go with me.
    In one respect I'll thy assistant be;
    For this alliance may so happy prove
    To turn your households' rancour to pure love.

Rom. O, let us hence! I stand on sudden haste.

Friar. Wisely, and slow. They stumble that run fast.
Exeunt.

Act Two, Scene Three Summary

Out in the road the following day, Benvolio discloses to Mercutio that Romeo has not yet get back. He additionally uncovers that Tybalt has sent Romeo a compromising message. At the point when Romeo goes along with them, Mercutio taunts him, however Romeo coordinates his mind. Intrigued, Mercutio notes,"Now craftsmanship thou friendly, presently workmanship thou Romeo" (2.3.77).

Scene IV. A street.

Enter Benvolio and Mercutio.

Mer. Where the devil should this Romeo be?
Came he not home to-night?

Ben. Not to his father's. I spoke with his man.

Mer. Why, that same pale hard-hearted wench, that Rosaline,
Torments him so that he will sure run mad.

Ben. Tybalt, the kinsman to old Capulet,
Hath sent a letter to his father's house.

Mer. A challenge, on my life.

Ben. Romeo will answer it.

Mer. Any man that can write may answer a letter.

Ben. Nay, he will answer the letter's master, how he dares, being dared.

Mer. Alas, poor Romeo, he is already dead! stabb'd with a white wench's black eye; shot through the ear with a love song; the very pin of his heart cleft with the blind bow-boy's butt-shaft; and is he a man to encounter Tybalt?

Ben. Why, what is Tybalt?

Mer. More than Prince of Cats, I can tell you. O, he's the courageous captain of compliments. He fights as you sing pricksong-keeps time, distance, and proportion; rests me his minim rest, one, two, and the third in your bosom! the very butcher of a silk button, a duellist, a duellist! a gentleman of the very first house, of the first and second cause. Ah, the immortal passado! the punto reverse! the hay.

Ben. The what?

Mer. The pox of such antic, lisping, affecting fantasticoes- these new tuners of accent! 'By Jesu, a very good blade! a very tall man! a very good whore!' Why, is not this a lamentable thing, grandsir, that we should be thus afflicted with these strange flies, these fashion-mongers, these pardona-mi's, who stand so much on the new form that they cannot sit at ease on the old bench? O, their bones, their bones!

Enter Romeo.

Ben. Here comes Romeo! here comes Romeo!

Mer. Without his roe, like a dried herring. O flesh, flesh, how art thou fishified! Now is he for the numbers that Petrarch flowed in. Laura, to his lady, was but a kitchen wench (marry, she had a better love to berhyme her), Dido a dowdy, Cleopatra a gypsy, Helen and Hero hildings and harlots, This be a gray eye or so, but not to the purpose. Signior Romeo, bon jour! There's a French salutation to your French slop. You gave us the counterfeit fairly last night.

Rom. Good morrow to you both. What counterfeit did I give you?

Mer. The slip, sir, the slip. Can you not conceive?

Rom. Pardon, good Mercutio. My business was great, and in such a
   case as mine a man may strain courtesy.

Mer. That's as much as to say, such a case as yours constrains a
   man to bow in the hams.

Rom. Meaning, to cursy.

Mer. Thou hast most kindly hit it.

Rom. A most courteous exposition.

Mer. Nay, I am the very pink of courtesy.

Rom. Pink for flower.

Mer. Right.

Rom. Why, then is my pump well-flower'd.

Mer. Well said! Follow me this jest now till thou hast worn out thy pump, that, when the single sole of it is worn, the jest may remain, after the wearing, solely singular.

Rom. O single-sold jest, solely singular for the singleness!

Mer. Come between us, good Benvolio! My wits faint.

Rom. Swits and spurs, swits and spurs! or I'll cry a match.

Mer. Nay, if our wits run the wild-goose chase, I am done; for thou hast more of the wild goose in one of thy wits than, I am sure, I have in my whole five. Was I with you there for the goose?

Rom. Thou wast never with me for anything when thou wast not there for the goose.

Mer. I will bite thee by the ear for that jest.

Rom. Nay, good goose, bite not!

Mer. Thy wit is a very bitter sweeting; it is a most sharp sauce.

Rom. And is it not, then, well serv'd in to a sweet goose?

  Mer. O, here's a wit of cheveril, that stretches from an inch
    narrow to an ell broad!

  Rom. I stretch it out for that word 'broad,' which, added to
    the goose, proves thee far and wide a broad goose.

Mer. Why, is not this better now than groaning for love? Now art thou sociable, now art thou Romeo; now art thou what thou art, by art as well as by nature. For this drivelling love is like a great natural that runs lolling up and down to hide his bauble in a hole.

Ben. Stop there, stop there!

Mer. Thou desirest me to stop in my tale against the hair.

Ben. Thou wouldst else have made thy tale large.

Mer. O, thou art deceiv'd! I would have made it short; for I was come to the whole depth of my tale, and meant indeed to occupy the argument no longer.

Rom. Here's goodly gear!

Enter Nurse and her Man [Peter].

Mer. A sail, a sail!

Ben. Two, two! a shirt and a smock.

Nurse. Peter!

Peter. Anon.

Nurse. My fan, Peter.

Mer. Good Peter, to hide her face; for her fan's the fairer face of the two.

Nurse. God ye good morrow, gentlemen.

Mer. God ye good-den, fair gentlewoman.

Nurse. Is it good-den?

Mer. 'Tis no less, I tell ye; for the bawdy hand of the dial is now upon the prick of noon.

Nurse. Out upon you! What a man are you!

Rom. One, gentlewoman, that God hath made for himself to mar.

Nurse. By my troth, it is well said. 'For himself to mar,' quoth 'a? Gentlemen, can any of you tell me where I may find the
    young Romeo?

Rom. I can tell you; but young Romeo will be older when you
    have found him than he was when you sought him. I am the youngest
    of that name, for fault of a worse.

Nurse. You say well.

Mer. Yea, is the worst well? Very well took, i' faith! wisely, wisely.

Nurse. If you be he, sir, I desire some confidence with you.

Ben. She will endite him to some supper.

Mer. A bawd, a bawd, a bawd! So ho!

Rom. What hast thou found?

Mer. No hare, sir; unless a hare, sir, in a lenten pie, that is
    something stale and hoar ere it be spent

He walks by them and sings.

An old hare hoar,
And an old hare hoar,
Is very good meat in Lent;
But a hare that is hoar
Is too much for a score
When it hoars ere it be spent.

Romeo, will you come to your father's? We'll to dinner thither.

Rom. I will follow you.

Mer. Farewell, ancient lady. Farewell,
  [sings] lady, lady, lady.
              Exeunt Mercutio, Benvolio.

Nurse. Marry, farewell! I Pray you, Sir, what saucy merchant
  was this that was so full of his ropery?

Rom. A gentleman, nurse, that loves to hear himself talk and
  will speak more in a minute than he will stand to in a month.

Nurse. An 'a speak anything against me, I'll take him down, an 'a
  were lustier than he is, and twenty such jacks; and if I cannot,
  I'll find those that shall. Scurvy knave! I am none of

his
 flirt-gills; I am none of his skains-mates. And thou must
 stand by too, and suffer every knave to use me at his pleasure!

Peter. I saw no man use you at his pleasure. If I had, my weapon should quickly have been out, I warrant you. I dare draw as soon as another man, if I see occasion in a good quarrel, and the law on my side.

Nurse. Now, afore God, I am so vexed that every part about me quivers. Scurvy knave! Pray you, sir, a word; and, as I told you, my young lady bid me enquire you out. What she bid me say, I will keep to myself; but first let me tell ye, if ye should lead her into a fool's paradise, as they say, it were a very gross kind of behaviour, as they say; for the gentlewoman is young; and therefore, if you should deal double with her, truly it were an ill thing to be off'red to any gentlewoman, and very weak dealing.

 Rom. Nurse, commend me to thy lady and mistress. I protest unto
 thee-

 Nurse. Good heart, and I faith I will tell her as much. Lord,
 Lord! she will be a joyful woman.

Rom. What wilt thou tell her, nurse? Thou dost not mark me.

Nurse. I will tell her, sir, that you do protest, which, as I take it, is a gentlemanlike offer.

Rom. Bid her devise
Some means to come to shrift this afternoon;
And there she shall at Friar Laurence' cell
Be shriv'd and married. Here is for thy pains.

Nurse. No, truly, sir; not a penny.

Rom. Go to! I say you shall.

Nurse. This afternoon, sir? Well, she shall be there.

Rom. And stay, good nurse, behind the abbey wall.
Within this hour my man shall be with thee
And bring thee cords made like a tackled stair,
Which to the high topgallant of my joy
Must be my convoy in the secret night.
Farewell. Be trusty, and I'll quit thy pains.
Farewell. Commend me to thy mistress.

Nurse. Now God in heaven bless thee! Hark you, sir.

Rom. What say'st thou, my dear nurse?

Nurse. Is your man secret? Did you ne'er hear say,
Two may keep counsel, putting one away?

Rom. I warrant thee my man's as true as steel.

Nurse. Well, sir, my mistress is the sweetest lady. Lord, Lord! when 'twas a little prating thing- O, there is a nobleman in town, one Paris, that would fain lay knife aboard; but she, good soul, had as lieve see a toad, a very toad, as see him. I anger her sometimes, and tell her that Paris is the properer man; but I'll warrant you, when I say so, she looks as pale as any clout in the versal world. Doth not rosemary and Romeo begin both with a letter?

Rom. Ay, nurse; what of that? Both with an R.

Nurse. Ah, mocker! that's the dog's name. R is for the- No; I know it begins with some other letter; and she hath the prettiest sententious of it, of you and rosemary, that it would do you good to hear it.

Rom. Commend me to thy lady.

Nurse. Ay, a thousand times. [Exit Romeo.] Peter!

Peter. Anon.

Nurse. Peter, take my fan, and go before, and apace.
Exeunt.

Act Two, Scene Four Summary

Back in the Capulet plantation, Juliet energetically anticipates news from the Nurse. At the point when the Nurse in the end shows up, she entertainingly will not give Juliet any data about Romeo until she has gotten a back rub. At long last, the Nurse enlightens Juliet regarding the arrangement for her to meet Romeo at Friar Laurence's church.

Scene V. Capulet's orchard.

Enter Juliet.

  Jul. The clock struck nine when I did send the nurse;
In half an hour she 'promis'd to return.
Perchance she cannot meet him. That's not so.
O, she is lame! Love's heralds should be thoughts,
Which ten times faster glide than the sun's beams
Driving back shadows over low'ring hills.
Therefore do nimble-pinion'd doves draw Love,
And therefore hath the wind-swift Cupid wings.
Now is the sun upon the highmost hill
Of this day's journey, and from nine till twelve
Is three long hours; yet she is not come.
Had she affections and warm youthful blood,
She would be as swift in motion as a ball;
My words would bandy her to my sweet love,
And his to me,
But old folks, many feign as they were dead-
Unwieldy, slow, heavy and pale as lead.

Enter Nurse [and Peter].

  O God, she comes! O honey nurse, what news?
Hast thou met with him? Send thy man away.

  Nurse. Peter, stay at the gate.
              [Exit Peter.]

  Jul. Now, good sweet nurse- O Lord, why look'st thou sad?
  Though news be sad, yet tell them merrily;
If good, thou shamest the music of sweet news

By playing it to me with so sour a face.

Nurse. I am aweary, give me leave awhile.
Fie, how my bones ache! What a jaunce have I had!

Jul. I would thou hadst my bones, and I thy news.
Nay, come, I pray thee speak. Good, good nurse, speak.

Nurse. Jesu, what haste! Can you not stay awhile?
Do you not see that I am out of breath?

Jul. How art thou out of breath when thou hast breath
To say to me that thou art out of breath?
The excuse that thou dost make in this delay
Is longer than the tale thou dost excuse.
Is thy news good or bad? Answer to that.
Say either, and I'll stay the circumstance.
Let me be satisfied, is't good or bad?

Nurse. Well, you have made a simple choice; you know not how to
choose a man. Romeo? No, not he. Though his face be better
than any man's, yet his leg excels all men's; and for a hand and a
foot, and a body, though they be not to be talk'd on, yet
they are past compare. He is not the flower of courtesy, but, I'll
warrant him, as gentle as a lamb. Go thy ways, wench; serve
God.

What, have you din'd at home?

Jul. No, no. But all this did I know before.
What says he of our marriage? What of that?

Nurse. Lord, how my head aches! What a head have I!
It beats as it would fall in twenty pieces.
My back o' t' other side,- ah, my back, my back!
Beshrew your heart for sending me about
To catch my death with jaucing up and down!

Jul. I' faith, I am sorry that thou art not well.
Sweet, sweet, Sweet nurse, tell me, what says my love?

Nurse. Your love says, like an honest gentleman, and a courteous,
and a kind, and a handsome; and, I warrant, a virtuous- Where
is your mother?

Jul. Where is my mother? Why, she is within.
Where should she be? How oddly thou repliest!
'Your love says, like an honest gentleman,
"Where is your mother?"'

Nurse. O God's Lady dear!
Are you so hot? Marry come up, I trow.
Is this the poultice for my aching bones?
Henceforward do your messages yourself.

Jul. Here's such a coil! Come, what says Romeo?

Nurse. Have you got leave to go to shrift to-day?

Jul. I have.

> Nurse. Then hie you hence to Friar Laurence' cell;
> There stays a husband to make you a wife.
> Now comes the wanton blood up in your cheeks:
> They'll be in scarlet straight at any news.
> Hie you to church; I must another way,
> To fetch a ladder, by the which your love
> Must climb a bird's nest soon when it is dark.
> I am the drudge, and toil in your delight;
> But you shall bear the burthen soon at night.
> Go; I'll to dinner; hie you to the cell.

Jul. Hie to high fortune! Honest nurse, farewell.
                                                Exeunt.

Act Two, Scene Five Summary

At the church, Romeo and Friar Laurence anticipate Juliet's appearance. The Friar alerts Romeo to "love tolerably" (2.5.9). Juliet before long shows up, and Friar Laurence carries them into the congregation to be hitched.

Scene VI. Friar Laurence's cell.

Enter Friar [Laurence] and Romeo.

Friar. So smile the heavens upon this holy act
That after-hours with sorrow chide us not!

Rom. Amen, amen! But come what sorrow can,
It cannot countervail the exchange of joy
That one short minute gives me in her sight.
Do thou but close our hands with holy words,
Then love-devouring death do what he dare-
It is enough I may but call her mine.

Friar. These violent delights have violent ends
And in their triumph die, like fire and powder,
Which, as they kiss, consume. The sweetest honey
Is loathsome in his own deliciousness
And in the taste confounds the appetite.
Therefore love moderately: long love doth so;
Too swift arrives as tardy as too slow.

Enter Juliet.

Here comes the lady. O, so light a foot
Will ne'er wear out the everlasting flint.
A lover may bestride the gossamer
That idles in the wanton summer air,
And yet not fall; so light is vanity.

Jul. Good even to my ghostly confessor.

Friar. Romeo shall thank thee, daughter, for us both.

Jul. As much to him, else is his thanks too much.

Rom. Ah, Juliet, if the measure of thy joy
Be heap'd like mine, and that thy skill be more

    To blazon it, then sweeten with thy breath
    This neighbour air, and let rich music's tongue
    Unfold the imagin'd happiness that both
    Receive in either by this dear encounter.

    Jul. Conceit, more rich in matter than in words,
    Brags of his substance, not of ornament.
    They are but beggars that can count their worth;
    But my true love is grown to such excess
    cannot sum up sum of half my wealth.

    Friar. Come, come with me, and we will make short work;
    For, by your leaves, you shall not stay alone
    Till Holy Church incorporate two in one.
                    [Exeunt.]

Act 2 Analysis

Act 2 is more engaged than Act 1, in that it for the most part serves to build up the marriage which will end up being the base of the play's sensational clash. Nonetheless, inside the streamlined plot, Shakespeare investigates the confusions of affection. The topic of affection is key to Act 2 of Romeo and Juliet. Romeo and Juliet begin to look all starry eyed at right away, and wed one day later, fixing their future. The overhang scene is essential to understanding their relationship since it permits Romeo and Juliet to test their underlying enthusiasm and increase the fearlessness to push ahead with a marriage plan.

The affection that Romeo and Juliet share is something contrary to the egotistical love that Shakespeare references in the initial demonstrations of the play. Shakespeare thinks about Juliet to the sun, and she is one of the most liberal characters in the play. She uncovers her benevolence when she pronounces, "My abundance is as limitless as the ocean,/My adoration as profound. The more I give thee/The more I have, for both are endless" (2.1.175-177). Rosaline, then again, wants to hush up about her excellence. Shakespeare increases this difference when Romeo portrays Rosaline as a Diana (the goddess of the moon) and tells Juliet, "Emerge, reasonable sun, and execute the desirous moon" (2.1.46).

In the overhang scene, Romeo and Juliet perceive this egotistical brand of adoration and afterward rise above it. The nursery setting is something beyond a mysterious gathering place – it conjures pictures of a peaceful Eden, which symbolizes both virtue and virginity. Romeo and Juliet's association is all the while established in unadulterated love and unbridled energy. Toward the start of the overhang scene, Romeo attacks Juliet's protection without her greeting, which turns out to be doubly obvious when he catches her talk. Here, Shakespeare breaks the show of the talk, which is customarily a discourse where a character shares their inward musings just with the crowd. That Romeo catches Juliet's monologue is an intrusion, on one hand, yet in addition fills in as a token of the expense of closeness. That Juliet both permits and values Romeo's interference reminds the crowd that genuine affection requires two individuals to hold nothing back from each other.

Shakespeare underscores that sweethearts must surrender their self-centeredness by having Romeo and Juliet promise to themselves, instead of to different bodies. For example, when Romeo attempts to depend on the moon, Juliet comments that the moon comes and goes, and is excessively factor. Rather, she says, "Or if thou shrivel, depend on thy generous self" (2.1.155). Shakespeare frequently has characters urge each other to be consistent with themselves solitary at that point would they be able to be consistent with others. On account of Romeo and Juliet, the characters must acknowledge their remarkable personalities (and rise above their family names) so as to encounter the most perfect sort of adoration.

Shakespeare likewise infers that when individuals begin to look all starry eyed at, they can develop. Juliet's conduct changes after she meets Romeo. She is accustomed to complying with the Nurse's position, and during the gallery scene, she vanishes twice. Notwithstanding, she additionally opposes authority twice so as to return and proceed with her discussion with Romeo. This is a certain indication of her rising autonomy, which discloses her fast choice to wed Romeo and resist her folks. Juliet additionally uncovers her down to earth knowledge by understanding the requirement for an arrangement for them to meet and by demanding marriage, which is an inversion of Elizabethan sex jobs. Romeo, while less dynamic than Juliet, likewise turns out to be progressively certain after their gathering, shunning his adolescent despairing for an increasingly gregarious character that dazzles Mercutio.

Shakespeare presents the subject of character in Act 2. In her speech, Juliet wishes that Romeo could rise above his name. Her acclaimed statement – "What's in a name? that which we call a rose/By some other name would smell as sweet" – communicates the possibility that individuals can be more than their cultural jobs. Juliet gets that on the off chance that she and Romeo are to be as one, they should oppose the constraints of society and follow their individual interests.

Right now, likewise presents Friar Laurence a multifaceted character who comprehends the requirement for individual self-governance. Due to his basic inspirations, be that as it may, the Friar is a blemished strict figure. He is eager to bargain the strict holiness of marriage for a political objective. He obviously discovers Romeo's new energy suspect, however consents to play out the wedding service with the goal that he can end the fight between the Montagues and Capulets. Minister Laurence's activities speak to the polarity between cultural show and individual want.

At long last, Shakespeare keeps on investigating the differentiations that he presented in Act I, especially the dissimilarity among night and day (or murkiness and light). Benvolio states, "Dazzle is his affection, and best befits the dim," in reference to Romeo's freshly discovered energy (2.1.32). When Romeo at long last observes Juliet at her gallery, he ponders, "However delicate, what light through there window breaks? /It is the east, and Juliet is the sun. /Arise, reasonable sun, and slaughter the jealous moon" (2.1.44-46). Romeo at that point conjures the murkiness as a type of security from hurt: "I have night's shroud to conceal me from their eyes" (2.1.117). Shockingly, the confusion of the day in the long run defeats the energetic and defensive night - obliterating the two sweethearts all the while.

Shakespeare additionally underlines the complexity among youth and mature age. Monk Laurence goes about as Romeo's comrade, and the Nurse exhorts Juliet. In any case, both these grown-ups offer counsel that appears to be unusually strange given the conditions of the play. For example, Friar Laurence says to Romeo, "Admirably and slow. They falter that run quick" (2.2.94). He additionally encourages Romeo to "Thusly love tolerably" (2.5.9). The Friar's guidance for Romeo to adore "tolerably", be that as it may, comes past the point of no return. Actually, before the finish of the play we even observe Friar Laurence dismissing his own recommendation and lurching to arrive at Juliet's grave before Romeo can discover her. "How oft this evening have my old feet lurched at graves?" (5.3.123).

At long last, Shakespeare presents the differentiation among silver and gold right now his utilization of symbolism. Romeo says, "How silver-sweet stable sweethearts' tongues around evening time" and "Woman, by there favored moon I promise,/That tips with silver all these organic product tree tops" (2.1.210, 149-50). Shakespeare frequently utilizes silver as an image of adoration and magnificence. Then again, he utilizes gold as an indication of ravenousness or want. Rosaline is insusceptible to showers of gold, a picture that summons the narrow-mindedness of renumeration. Afterward, when Romeo is exiled, he remarks that expulsion is a "brilliant hatchet," implying that his discipline is only a bypassed likeness passing. Lastly, the erection of the brilliant statues toward the end an indication of the way that neither Capulet nor Montague has truly taken in anything from Romeo and Juliet's demises.

ACT III. Scene I. A public place.

Enter Mercutio, Benvolio, and Men.

Ben. I pray thee, good Mercutio, let's retire.
The day is hot, the Capulets abroad.
And if we meet, we shall not scape a brawl,
For now, these hot days, is the mad blood stirring.

Mer. Thou art like one of these fellows that, when he enters
   the confines of a tavern, claps me his sword upon the table and
   says 'God send me no need of thee!' and by the operation of the
   second cup draws him on the drawer, when indeed there is no need.

Ben. Am I like such a fellow?

Mer. Come, come, thou art as hot a jack in thy mood as any in
   Italy; and as soon moved to be moody, and as soon moody to be
   moved.

Ben. And what to?

Mer. Nay, an there were two such, we should have none shortly, for one would kill the other. Thou! why, thou wilt quarrel with a man that hath a hair more or a hair less in his beard than thou hast. Thou wilt quarrel with a man for cracking nuts, having no other reason but because thou hast hazel eyes. What eye but such an eye would spy out such a quarrel? Thy head is as full of quarrels as an egg is full of meat; and yet thy head hath been beaten as addle as an egg for quarrelling. Thou hast quarrell'd with a man for coughing in the street, because he hath wakened thy dog that hath lain asleep in the sun. Didst thou not fall out with a tailor for wearing his new doublet before Easter, with another for tying his new shoes with an old riband? And yet thou wilt tutor me from quarrelling!

Ben. An I were so apt to quarrel as thou art, any man should buy the fee simple of my life for an hour and a quarter.

Mer. The fee simple? O simple!

Enter Tybalt and others.

Ben. By my head, here come the Capulets.

Mer. By my heel, I care not.

  Tyb. Follow me close, for I will speak to them.
    Gentlemen, good den. A word with one of you.

  Mer. And but one word with one of us?
    Couple it with something; make it a word and a blow.

  Tyb. You shall find me apt enough to that, sir, an you will give me
    occasion.

Mer. Could you not take some occasion without giving

Tyb. Mercutio, thou consortest with Romeo.

Mer. Consort? What, dost thou make us minstrels? An thou make
   minstrels of us, look to hear nothing but discords. Here's my
   fiddlestick; here's that shall make you dance. Zounds, consort!

Ben. We talk here in the public haunt of men.
   Either withdraw unto some private place
   And reason coldly of your grievances,
   Or else depart. Here all eyes gaze on us.

Mer. Men's eyes were made to look, and let them gaze.
   I will not budge for no man's pleasure,

Enter Romeo.

Tyb. Well, peace be with you, sir. Here comes my man.

Mer. But I'll be hang'd, sir, if he wear your livery.
   Marry, go before to field, he'll be your follower!
   Your worship in that sense may call him man.

Tyb. Romeo, the love I bear thee can afford
   No better term than this: thou art a villain.

Rom. Tybalt, the reason that I have to love thee
   Doth much excuse the appertaining rage
   To such a greeting. Villain am I none.
   Therefore farewell. I see thou knowest me not.

Tyb. Boy, this shall not excuse the injuries
That thou hast done me; therefore turn and draw.

Rom. I do protest I never injur'd thee,
But love thee better than thou canst devise
Till thou shalt know the reason of my love;
And so good Capulet, which name I tender
As dearly as mine own, be satisfied.

Mer. O calm, dishonourable, vile submission!
Alla stoccata carries it away. [Draws.]
Tybalt, you ratcatcher, will you walk?

Tyb. What wouldst thou have with me?

Mer. Good King of Cats, nothing but one of your nine lives.
That I
mean to make bold withal, and, as you shall use me hereafter,

dry-beat the rest of the eight. Will you pluck your sword out
of his pitcher by the ears? Make haste, lest mine be about your
ears ere it be out.

Tyb. I am for you. [Draws.]

Rom. Gentle Mercutio, put thy rapier up.

Mer. Come, sir, your passado!
[They fight.]

Rom. Draw, Benvolio; beat down their weapons.
Gentlemen, for shame! forbear this outrage!
Tybalt, Mercutio, the Prince expressly hath
Forbid this bandying in Verona streets.
Hold, Tybalt! Good Mercutio!
    Tybalt under Romeo's arm thrusts Mercutio in, and flies
            [with his Followers].

Mer. I am hurt.
A plague o' both your houses! I am sped.
Is he gone and hath nothing?

Ben. What, art thou hurt?

Mer. Ay, ay, a scratch, a scratch. Marry, 'tis enough.
Where is my page? Go, villain, fetch a surgeon.
            [Exit Page.]

Rom. Courage, man. The hurt cannot be much.

Mer. No, 'tis not so deep as a well, nor so wide as a church door;
    but 'tis enough, 'twill serve. Ask for me to-morrow, and you
    shall find me a grave man. I am peppered, I warrant, for this
    world. A plague o' both your houses! Zounds, a dog, a rat, a
    mouse, a cat, to scratch a man to death! a braggart, a

rogue,
a
   villain, that fights by the book of arithmetic! Why the devil
   came you between us? I was hurt under your arm.

Rom. I thought all for the best.

  Mer. Help me into some house, Benvolio,
    Or I shall faint. A plague o' both your houses!
    They have made worms' meat of me. I have it,
    And soundly too. Your houses!
              [Exit. [supported by Benvolio].

  Rom. This gentleman, the Prince's near ally,
    My very friend, hath got this mortal hurt
    In my behalf- my reputation stain'd
    With Tybalt's slander- Tybalt, that an hour
    Hath been my kinsman. O sweet Juliet,
    Thy beauty hath made me effeminate
    And in my temper soft'ned valour's steel

Enter Benvolio.

  Ben. O Romeo, Romeo, brave Mercutio's dead!
    That gallant spirit hath aspir'd the clouds,
    Which too untimely here did scorn the earth.

  Rom. This day's black fate on moe days doth depend;
    This but begins the woe others must end.

Enter Tybalt.

Ben. Here comes the furious Tybalt back again.

Rom. Alive in triumph, and Mercutio slain?
Away to heaven respective lenity,
And fire-ey'd fury be my conduct now!
Now, Tybalt, take the 'villain' back again
That late thou gavest me; for Mercutio's soul
Is but a little way above our heads,
Staying for thine to keep him company.
Either thou or I, or both, must go with him.

Tyb. Thou, wretched boy, that didst consort him here,
Shalt with him hence.

Rom. This shall determine that.
They fight. Tybalt falls.

Ben. Romeo, away, be gone!
The citizens are up, and Tybalt slain.
Stand not amaz'd. The Prince will doom thee death
If thou art taken. Hence, be gone, away!

Rom. O, I am fortune's fool!

Ben. Why dost thou stay?
Exit Romeo.
Enter Citizens.

Citizen. Which way ran he that kill'd Mercutio?
Tybalt, that murtherer, which way ran he?

Ben. There lies that Tybalt.

Citizen. Up, sir, go with me.
I charge thee in the Prince's name obey.

Enter Prince [attended], Old Montague, Capulet, their Wives,
         and [others].

Prince. Where are the vile beginners of this fray?

Ben. O noble Prince. I can discover all
  The unlucky manage of this fatal brawl.
  There lies the man, slain by young Romeo,
  That slew thy kinsman, brave Mercutio.

Cap. Wife. Tybalt, my cousin! O my brother's child!
O Prince! O husband! O, the blood is spill'd
Of my dear kinsman! Prince, as thou art true,
For blood of ours shed blood of Montague.
O cousin, cousin!

Prince. Benvolio, who began this bloody fray?

Ben. Tybalt, here slain, whom Romeo's hand did stay.
  Romeo, that spoke him fair, bid him bethink
  How nice the quarrel was, and urg'd withal
  Your high displeasure. All this- uttered
  With gentle breath, calm look, knees humbly bow'd-
  Could not take truce with the unruly spleen
  Of Tybalt deaf to peace, but that he tilts
  With piercing steel at bold Mercutio's breast;
  Who, all as hot, turns deadly point to point,
  And, with a martial scorn, with one hand beats
  Cold death aside and with the other sends

It back to Tybalt, whose dexterity
Retorts it. Romeo he cries aloud,
'Hold, friends! friends, part!' and swifter than his tongue,
His agile arm beats down their fatal points,
And 'twixt them rushes; underneath whose arm
An envious thrust from Tybalt hit the life
Of stout Mercutio, and then Tybalt fled;
But by-and-by comes back to Romeo,
Who had but newly entertain'd revenge,
And to't they go like lightning; for, ere I
Could draw to part them, was stout Tybalt slain;
And, as he fell, did Romeo turn and fly.
This is the truth, or let Benvolio die.

Cap. Wife. He is a kinsman to the Montague;
Affection makes him false, he speaks not true.
Some twenty of them fought in this black strife,
And all those twenty could but kill one life.
I beg for justice, which thou, Prince, must give.
Romeo slew Tybalt; Romeo must not live.

Prince. Romeo slew him; he slew Mercutio.
Who now the price of his dear blood doth owe?

Mon. Not Romeo, Prince; he was Mercutio's friend;
His fault concludes but what the law should end,
The life of Tybalt.

Prince. And for that offence
Immediately we do exile him hence.
I have an interest in your hate's proceeding,
My blood for your rude brawls doth lie a-bleeding;

But I'll amerce you with so strong a fine
That you shall all repent the loss of mine.
I will be deaf to pleading and excuses;
Nor tears nor prayers shall purchase out abuses.
Therefore use none. Let Romeo hence in haste,
Else, when he is found, that hour is his last.
Bear hence this body, and attend our will.
Mercy but murders, pardoning those that kill.
      Exeunt.

Act Three, Scene One Summary

Outside on the Verona road, Benvolio and Mercutio look out for Romeo to meet them. Tybalt and Petruccio see them first, and start a squabble. Tybalt clarifies that he is searching for Romeo, whom he needs to rebuff for sneaking into the Capulets' conceal party the earlier day.

At the point when Romeo shows up, thrilled with his ongoing marriage, he is respectful to Tybalt, demanding he harbors no scorn for the Capulet house. Tybalt is uncertain how to manage Romeo. Be that as it may, Mercutio challenges Tybalt to a duel, so he draws his sword and assaults Mercutio. Romeo endeavors to mediate, keeping Mercutio down. While Romeo is limiting him, Tybalt wounds Mercutio and afterward exits rapidly.

Mercutio is mortally injured, and chastens the Montagues and Capulets for empowering such savagery previously permitting Benvolio to lead him offstage. Benvolio before long comes back with news that Mercutio has kicked the bucket. Romeo pledges retribution on Tybalt, who before long returns. Romeo and Tybalt duel, and Romeo executes Tybalt. He at that point escapes rapidly after Benvolio cautions him that the Prince will come soon.

The Prince, trailed by the Montague and Capulet families, shows up on the scene. Benvolio reveals to him the whole story, yet the Prince will not hold Romeo faultless. Rather, he ousts Romeo from Verona, demanding the kid will kick the bucket on the off chance that he doesn't comply.

Scene II. Capulet's orchard.

Enter Juliet alone.

Jul. Gallop apace, you fiery-footed steeds,
   Towards Phoebus' lodging! Such a wagoner
   As Phaeton would whip you to the West
   And bring in cloudy night immediately.
   Spread thy close curtain, love-performing night,
   That runaway eyes may wink, and Romeo
   Leap to these arms untalk'd of and unseen.
   Lovers can see to do their amorous rites
   By their own beauties; or, if love be blind,
   It best agrees with night. Come, civil night,
   Thou sober-suited matron, all in black,
   And learn me how to lose a winning match,
   Play'd for a pair of stainless maidenhoods.
   Hood my unmann'd blood, bating in my cheeks,
   With thy black mantle till strange love, grown bold,
   Think true love acted simple modesty.
   Come, night; come, Romeo; come, thou day in night;
   For thou wilt lie upon the wings of night
   Whiter than new snow upon a raven's back.
   Come, gentle night; come, loving, black-brow'd night;

Give me my Romeo; and, when he shall die,
Take him and cut him out in little stars,
And he will make the face of heaven so fine
That all the world will be in love with night
And pay no worship to the garish sun.
O, I have bought the mansion of a love,
But not possess'd it; and though I am sold,
Not yet enjoy'd. So tedious is this day
As is the night before some festival
To an impatient child that hath new robes
And may not wear them. O, here comes my nurse,

Enter Nurse, with cords.

And she brings news; and every tongue that speaks
But Romeo's name speaks heavenly eloquence.
Now, nurse, what news? What hast thou there? the cords
That Romeo bid thee fetch?

Nurse. Ay, ay, the cords.
[Throws them down.]

Jul. Ay me! what news? Why dost thou wring thy hands

Nurse. Ah, weraday! he's dead, he's dead, he's dead!
We are undone, lady, we are undone!
Alack the day! he's gone, he's kill'd, he's dead!

Jul. Can heaven be so envious?

Nurse. Romeo can,
Though heaven cannot. O Romeo, Romeo!

Who ever would have thought it? Romeo!

Jul. What devil art thou that dost torment me thus?
This torture should be roar'd in dismal hell.
Hath Romeo slain himself? Say thou but 'I,'
And that bare vowel 'I' shall poison more
Than the death-darting eye of cockatrice.
I am not I, if there be such an 'I';
Or those eyes shut that make thee answer 'I.'
If be be slain, say 'I'; or if not, 'no.'
Brief sounds determine of my weal or woe.

Nurse. I saw the wound, I saw it with mine eyes,
(God save the mark!) here on his manly breast.
A piteous corse, a bloody piteous corse;
Pale, pale as ashes, all bedaub'd in blood,
All in gore-blood. I swounded at the sight.

Jul. O, break, my heart! poor bankrout, break at once!
To prison, eyes; ne'er look on liberty!
Vile earth, to earth resign; end motion here,
And thou and Romeo press one heavy bier!

Nurse. O Tybalt, Tybalt, the best friend I had!
O courteous Tybalt! honest gentleman
That ever I should live to see thee dead!

Jul. What storm is this that blows so contrary?
Is Romeo slaught'red, and is Tybalt dead?
My dear-lov'd cousin, and my dearer lord?
Then, dreadful trumpet, sound the general doom!

For who is living, if those two are gone?

Nurse. Tybalt is gone, and Romeo banished;
Romeo that kill'd him, he is banished.

Jul. O God! Did Romeo's hand shed Tybalt's blood?

Nurse. It did, it did! alas the day, it did!

Jul. O serpent heart, hid with a flow'ring face!
Did ever dragon keep so fair a cave?
Beautiful tyrant! fiend angelical!
Dove-feather'd raven! wolvish-ravening lamb!
Despised substance of divinest show!
Just opposite to what thou justly seem'st-
A damned saint, an honourable villain!
O nature, what hadst thou to do in hell
When thou didst bower the spirit of a fiend
In mortal paradise of such sweet flesh?
Was ever book containing such vile matter
So fairly bound? O, that deceit should dwell
In such a gorgeous palace!

Nurse. There's no trust,
No faith, no honesty in men; all perjur'd,
All forsworn, all naught, all dissemblers.
Ah, where's my man? Give me some aqua vitae.
These griefs, these woes, these sorrows make me old.
Shame come to Romeo!

Jul. Blister'd be thy tongue
For such a wish! He was not born to shame.
Upon his brow shame is asham'd to sit;

For 'tis a throne where honour may be crown'd
Sole monarch of the universal earth.
O, what a beast was I to chide at him!

Nurse. Will you speak well of him that kill'd your cousin?

Jul. Shall I speak ill of him that is my husband?
  Ah, poor my lord, what tongue shall smooth thy name
  When I, thy three-hours wife, have mangled it?
  But wherefore, villain, didst thou kill my cousin?
  That villain cousin would have kill'd my husband.
  Back, foolish tears, back to your native spring!
  Your tributary drops belong to woe,
  Which you, mistaking, offer up to joy.
  My husband lives, that Tybalt would have slain;
  And Tybalt's dead, that would have slain my husband.
  All this is comfort; wherefore weep I then?
  Some word there was, worser than Tybalt's death,
  That murd'red me. I would forget it fain;
  But O, it presses to my memory
  Like damned guilty deeds to sinners' minds!
  'Tybalt is dead, and Romeo- banished.'
  That 'banished,' that one word 'banished,'
  Hath slain ten thousand Tybalts. Tybalt's death
  Was woe enough, if it had ended there;
  Or, if sour woe delights in fellowship
  And needly will be rank'd with other griefs,
  Why followed not, when she said 'Tybalt's dead,'
  Thy father, or thy mother, nay, or both,
  Which modern lamentation might have mov'd?
  But with a rearward following Tybalt's death,
  'Romeo is banished'- to speak that word
  Is father, mother, Tybalt, Romeo, Juliet,
  All slain, all dead. 'Romeo is banished'-

There is no end, no limit, measure, bound,
In that word's death; no words can that woe sound.
Where is my father and my mother, nurse?

Nurse. Weeping and wailing over Tybalt's corse.
Will you go to them? I will bring you thither.

Jul. Wash they his wounds with tears? Mine shall be spent,
When theirs are dry, for Romeo's banishment.
Take up those cords. Poor ropes, you are beguil'd,
Both you and I, for Romeo is exil'd.
He made you for a highway to my bed;
But I, a maid, die maiden-widowed.
Come, cords; come, nurse. I'll to my wedding bed;
And death, not Romeo, take my maidenhead!

Nurse. Hie to your chamber. I'll find Romeo
To comfort you. I wot well where he is.
Hark ye, your Romeo will be here at night.
I'll to him; he is hid at Laurence' cell.

Jul. O, find him! give this ring to my true knight
And bid him come to take his last farewell.
                              Exeunt.

Act Three, Scene Two Summary

As she trusts that Romeo will show up, Juliet conveys one of the play's most exquisite discourses about her dearest. The Nurse enters, upset and talking vaguely; Juliet can just perceive that somebody has passed on and that somebody has been expelled. As she did in the past scene, the Nurse won't reveal to Juliet what she knows. Rather, she permits Juliet to accept that it is Romeo who has been executed.

At the point when the Nurse at long last uncovers reality, Juliet promptly rebukes Romeo over his misrepresentation of harmony and opposing viciousness. She at that point abnegates the allegation, and asks the Nurse, "Will I tear down him that is my significant other?" (3.2.97). Survive, Juliet regrets Romeo's expulsion, and cases that she would prefer to have both her folks murdered at that point see Romeo endure such outrage.

The Nurse vows to discover Romeo – whom she knows is covering up with Friar Laurence - and carry him to Juliet's bed that night. Juliet gives the Nurse a ring for Romeo to wear when he comes to see her.

Scene III. Friar Laurence's cell.

Enter Friar [Laurence].

> Friar. Romeo, come forth; come forth, thou fearful man.
> Affliction is enanmour'd of thy parts,
> And thou art wedded to calamity.

Enter Romeo.

Rom. Father, what news? What is the Prince's doom
What sorrow craves acquaintance at my hand
That I yet know not?

Friar. Too familiar
Is my dear son with such sour company.
I bring thee tidings of the Prince's doom.

Rom. What less than doomsday is the Prince's doom?

Friar. A gentler judgment vanish'd from his lips-
Not body's death, but body's banishment.

Rom. Ha, banishment? Be merciful, say 'death';
For exile hath more terror in his look,
Much more than death. Do not say 'banishment.'

Friar. Hence from Verona art thou banished.
Be patient, for the world is broad and wide.

Rom. There is no world without Verona walls,
But purgatory, torture, hell itself.
Hence banished is banish'd from the world,
And world's exile is death. Then 'banishment'
Is death misterm'd. Calling death 'banishment,'
Thou cut'st my head off with a golden axe
And smilest upon the stroke that murders me.

Friar. O deadly sin! O rude unthankfulness!
Thy fault our law calls death; but the kind Prince,
Taking thy part, hath rush'd aside the law,
And turn'd that black word death to banishment.

This is dear mercy, and thou seest it not.

Rom. 'Tis torture, and not mercy. Heaven is here,
Where Juliet lives; and every cat and dog
And little mouse, every unworthy thing,
Live here in heaven and may look on her;
But Romeo may not. More validity,
More honourable state, more courtship lives
In carrion flies than Romeo. They may seize
On the white wonder of dear Juliet's hand
And steal immortal blessing from her lips,
Who, even in pure and vestal modesty,
Still blush, as thinking their own kisses sin;
But Romeo may not- he is banished.
This may flies do, when I from this must fly;
They are free men, but I am banished.
And sayest thou yet that exile is not death?
Hadst thou no poison mix'd, no sharp-ground knife,
No sudden mean of death, though ne'er so mean,
But 'banished' to kill me- 'banished'?
O friar, the damned use that word in hell;
Howling attends it! How hast thou the heart,
Being a divine, a ghostly confessor,
A sin-absolver, and my friend profess'd,
To mangle me with that word 'banished'?

Friar. Thou fond mad man, hear me a little speak.

Rom. O, thou wilt speak again of banishment.

Friar. I'll give thee armour to keep off that word;
Adversity's sweet milk, philosophy,
To comfort thee, though thou art banished.

Rom. Yet 'banished'? Hang up philosophy!
Unless philosophy can make a Juliet,
Displant a town, reverse a prince's doom,
It helps not, it prevails not. Talk no more.

Friar. O, then I see that madmen have no ears.

Rom. How should they, when that wise men have no eyes?

Friar. Let me dispute with thee of thy estate.

Rom. Thou canst not speak of that thou dost not feel.
Wert thou as young as I, Juliet thy love,
An hour but married, Tybalt murdered,
Doting like me, and like me banished,
Then mightst thou speak, then mightst thou tear thy hair,
And fall upon the ground, as I do now,
Taking the measure of an unmade grave.
                    Knock [within].

Friar. Arise; one knocks. Good Romeo, hide thyself.

Rom. Not I; unless the breath of heartsick groans,
Mist-like infold me from the search of eyes. Knock.

Friar. Hark, how they knock! Who's there? Romeo, arise;
Thou wilt be taken.- Stay awhile!- Stand up; Knock.
Run to my study.- By-and-by!- God's will,
What simpleness is this.- I come, I come! Knock.
Who knocks so hard? Whence come you? What's your will

Nurse. [within] Let me come in, and you shall know my errand.
  I come from Lady Juliet.

Friar. Welcome then.

Enter Nurse.

Nurse. O holy friar, O, tell me, holy friar
  Where is my lady's lord, where's Romeo?

Friar. There on the ground, with his own tears made drunk.

Nurse. O, he is even in my mistress' case,
  Just in her case!

Friar. O woeful sympathy!
  Piteous predicament!

Nurse. Even so lies she,
  Blubb'ring and weeping, weeping and blubbering.
  Stand up, stand up! Stand, an you be a man.
  For Juliet's sake, for her sake, rise and stand!
  Why should you fall into so deep an O?

Rom. (rises) Nurse—

Nurse. Ah sir! ah sir! Well, death's the end of all.

Rom. Spakest thou of Juliet? How is it with her?
  Doth not she think me an old murtherer,
  Now I have stain'd the childhood of our joy
  With blood remov'd but little from her own?

Where is she? and how doth she! and what says
My conceal'd lady to our cancell'd love?

Nurse. O, she says nothing, sir, but weeps and weeps;
And now falls on her bed, and then starts up,
And Tybalt calls; and then on Romeo cries,
And then down falls again.

Rom. As if that name,
Shot from the deadly level of a gun,
Did murther her; as that name's cursed hand
Murder'd her kinsman. O, tell me, friar, tell me,
In what vile part of this anatomy
Doth my name lodge? Tell me, that I may sack
The hateful mansion. [Draws his dagger.]

Friar. Hold thy desperate hand.
Art thou a man? Thy form cries out thou art;
Thy tears are womanish, thy wild acts denote
The unreasonable fury of a beast.
Unseemly woman in a seeming man!
Or ill-beseeming beast in seeming both!
Thou hast amaz'd me. By my holy order,
I thought thy disposition better temper'd.
Hast thou slain Tybalt? Wilt thou slay thyself?
And slay thy lady that in thy life lives,
By doing damned hate upon thyself?
Why railest thou on thy birth, the heaven, and earth?
Since birth and heaven and earth, all three do meet
In thee at once; which thou at once wouldst lose.
Fie, fie, thou shamest thy shape, thy love, thy wit,
Which, like a usurer, abound'st in all,
And usest none in that true use indeed

Which should bedeck thy shape, thy love, thy wit.
Thy noble shape is but a form of wax
Digressing from the valour of a man;
Thy dear love sworn but hollow perjury,
Killing that love which thou hast vow'd to cherish;
Thy wit, that ornament to shape and love,
Misshapen in the conduct of them both,
Like powder in a skilless soldier's flask,
is get afire by thine own ignorance,
And thou dismemb'red with thine own defence.
What, rouse thee, man! Thy Juliet is alive,
For whose dear sake thou wast but lately dead.
There art thou happy. Tybalt would kill thee,
But thou slewest Tybalt. There art thou happy too.
The law, that threat'ned death, becomes thy friend
And turns it to exile. There art thou happy.
A pack of blessings light upon thy back;
Happiness courts thee in her best array;
But, like a misbhav'd and sullen wench,
Thou pout'st upon thy fortune and thy love.
Take heed, take heed, for such die miserable.
Go get thee to thy love, as was decreed,
Ascend her chamber, hence and comfort her.
But look thou stay not till the watch be set,
For then thou canst not pass to Mantua,
Where thou shalt live till we can find a time
To blaze your marriage, reconcile your friends,
Beg pardon of the Prince, and call thee back
With twenty hundred thousand times more joy
Than thou went'st forth in lamentation.
Go before, nurse. Commend me to thy lady,
And bid her hasten all the house to bed,
Which heavy sorrow makes them apt unto.
Romeo is coming.

Nurse. O Lord, I could have stay'd here all the night
To hear good counsel. O, what learning is!
My lord, I'll tell my lady you will come.

Rom. Do so, and bid my sweet prepare to chide.

Nurse. Here is a ring she bid me give you, sir.
Hie you, make haste, for it grows very late. Exit.

Rom. How well my comfort is reviv'd by this!

Friar. Go hence; good night; and here stands all your state:
Either be gone before the watch be set,
Or by the break of day disguis'd from hence.
Sojourn in Mantua. I'll find out your man,
And he shall signify from time to time
Every good hap to you that chances here.
Give me thy hand. 'Tis late. Farewell; good night.

Rom. But that a joy past joy calls out on me,
It were a grief so brief to part with thee.
Farewell.
        Exeunt.

Act Three, Scene Three Summary

In the house of prayer, where Romeo is stowing away, Friar Laurence illuminates the kid about his discipline, including that he ought to be upbeat that the Prince drove capital punishment. Romeo looks at expulsion as a deplorable outcome, since it will isolate him from his cherished Juliet. At the point when the Friar attempts to comfort him, Romeo says, "Wert thou as youthful as I, Juliet thy love.../Then mightst thou talk" (3.3.65-68).

The Nurse shows up to discover Romeo fallen on the ground, sobbing. She arranges him to stand, yet he is vexed to the point that he plans to wound himself. She grabs away his blade, and Friar Laurence asks Romeo to take a gander at the brilliant side - at any rate he and Juliet are both still alive. The Friar at that point persuades Romeo to visit Juliet that night, and to run away to Mantua toward the beginning of the day.

Scene IV. Capulet's house

Enter Old Capulet, his Wife, and Paris.

  Cap. Things have fall'n out, sir, so unluckily
    That we have had no time to move our daughter.
    Look you, she lov'd her kinsman Tybalt dearly,
    And so did I. Well, we were born to die.
    'Tis very late; she'll not come down to-night.
    I promise you, but for your company,
    I would have been abed an hour ago.

  Par. These times of woe afford no tune to woo.
    Madam, good night. Commend me to your daughter.

Lady. I will, and know her mind early to-morrow;
To-night she's mew'd up to her heaviness.

Cap. Sir Paris, I will make a desperate tender
Of my child's love. I think she will be rul'd
In all respects by me; nay more, I doubt it not.
Wife, go you to her ere you go to bed;
Acquaint her here of my son Paris' love
And bid her (mark you me?) on Wednesday next-
But, soft! what day is this?

Par. Monday, my lord.

Cap. Monday! ha, ha! Well, Wednesday is too soon.
Thursday let it be- a Thursday, tell her
She shall be married to this noble earl.
Will you be ready? Do you like this haste?
We'll keep no great ado- a friend or two;
For hark you, Tybalt being slain so late,
It may be thought we held him carelessly,
Being our kinsman, if we revel much.
Therefore we'll have some half a dozen friends,
And there an end. But what say you to Thursday?

Par. My lord, I would that Thursday were to-morrow.

Cap. Well, get you gone. A Thursday be it then.
Go you to Juliet ere you go to bed;
Prepare her, wife, against this wedding day.
Farewell, My lord.- Light to my chamber, ho!
Afore me, It is so very very late
That we may call it early by-and-by.
Good night.

Exeunt

Act Three, Scene Four Summary

At the Capulet family, the senior Capulets and Paris plan for bed; they have been up the entire evening grieving Tybalt's demise. They talk about Juliet's outrageous hopelessness which they accept to be the consequence of losing her cousin, Tybalt.

Incompletely in light of the fact that he trusts it will mitigate her bitterness, Lord Capulet chooses right then that Juliet will wed Paris, and that the wedding will occur soon thereafter. He remarks, "I figure she will be administered/In all regards by me" (3.4.13-14). He arranges Lady Capulet to illuminate Juliet about the issue, and afterward leaves for bed.

Scene V. Capulet's orchard.

Enter Romeo and Juliet aloft, at the Window.

Jul. Wilt thou be gone? It is not yet near day.
  It was the nightingale, and not the lark,
  That pierc'd the fearful hollow of thine ear.
  Nightly she sings on yond pomegranate tree.
  Believe me, love, it was the nightingale.

Rom. It was the lark, the herald of the morn;
  No nightingale. Look, love, what envious streaks
  Do lace the severing clouds in yonder East.
  Night's candles are burnt out, and jocund day
  Stands tiptoe on the misty mountain tops.
  I must be gone and live, or stay and die.

Jul. Yond light is not daylight; I know it, I.
It is some meteor that the sun exhales
To be to thee this night a torchbearer
And light thee on the way to Mantua.
Therefore stay yet; thou need'st not to be gone.

Rom. Let me be ta'en, let me be put to death.
I am content, so thou wilt have it so.
I'll say yon grey is not the morning's eye,
'Tis but the pale reflex of Cynthia's brow;
Nor that is not the lark whose notes do beat
The vaulty heaven so high above our heads.
I have more care to stay than will to go.
Come, death, and welcome! Juliet wills it so.
How is't, my soul? Let's talk; it is not day.

Jul. It is, it is! Hie hence, be gone, away!
It is the lark that sings so out of tune,
Straining harsh discords and unpleasing sharps.
Some say the lark makes sweet division;
This doth not so, for she divideth us.
Some say the lark and loathed toad chang'd eyes;
O, now I would they had chang'd voices too,
Since arm from arm that voice doth us affray,
Hunting thee hence with hunt's-up to the day!
O, now be gone! More light and light it grows.

Rom. More light and light- more dark and dark our woes!

Enter Nurse.

Nurse. Madam!

Jul. Nurse?

Nurse. Your lady mother is coming to your chamber.
The day is broke; be wary, look about.

Jul. Then, window, let day in, and let life out.
[Exit.]

Rom. Farewell, farewell! One kiss, and I'll descend.
He goeth down.

Jul. Art thou gone so, my lord, my love, my friend?
I must hear from thee every day in the hour,
For in a minute there are many days.
O, by this count I shall be much in years
Ere I again behold my Romeo!

Rom. Farewell!
I will omit no opportunity
That may convey my greetings, love, to thee.

Jul. O, think'st thou we shall ever meet again?

Rom. I doubt it not; and all these woes shall serve
For sweet discourses in our time to come.

Jul. O God, I have an ill-divining soul!
Methinks I see thee, now thou art below,
As one dead in the bottom of a tomb.
Either my eyesight fails, or thou look'st pale.

Rom. And trust me, love, in my eye so do you.
Dry sorrow drinks our blood. Adieu, adieu!
Exit.

Jul. O Fortune, Fortune! all men call thee fickle.
If thou art fickle, what dost thou with him
That is renown'd for faith? Be fickle, Fortune,
For then I hope thou wilt not keep him long
But send him back.

Lady. [within] Ho, daughter! are you up?

Jul. Who is't that calls? It is my lady mother.
Is she not down so late, or up so early?
What unaccustom'd cause procures her hither?

Enter Mother.

Lady. Why, how now, Juliet?

Jul. Madam, I am not well.

Lady. Evermore weeping for your cousin's death?
What, wilt thou wash him from his grave with tears?
An if thou couldst, thou couldst not make him live.
Therefore have done. Some grief shows much of love;
But much of grief shows still some want of wit.

Jul. Yet let me weep for such a feeling loss.

Lady. So shall you feel the loss, but not the friend
Which you weep for.

Jul. Feeling so the loss,
   I cannot choose but ever weep the friend.

Lady. Well, girl, thou weep'st not so much for his death
   As that the villain lives which slaughter'd him.

Jul. What villain, madam?

Lady. That same villain Romeo.

Jul. [aside] Villain and he be many miles asunder.-
   God pardon him! I do, with all my heart;
   And yet no man like he doth grieve my heart.

Lady. That is because the traitor murderer lives.

Jul. Ay, madam, from the reach of these my hands.
   Would none but I might venge my cousin's death!

Lady. We will have vengeance for it, fear thou not.
   Then weep no more. I'll send to one in Mantua,
   Where that same banish'd runagate doth live,
   Shall give him such an unaccustom'd dram
   That he shall soon keep Tybalt company;
   And then I hope thou wilt be satisfied.

Jul. Indeed I never shall be satisfied
   With Romeo till I behold him- dead-
   Is my poor heart so for a kinsman vex'd.
   Madam, if you could find out but a man
   To bear a poison, I would temper it;
   That Romeo should, upon receipt thereof,
   Soon sleep in quiet. O, how my heart abhors

 To hear him nam'd and cannot come to him,
To wreak the love I bore my cousin Tybalt
Upon his body that hath slaughter'd him!

 Lady. Find thou the means, and I'll find such a man.
But now I'll tell thee joyful tidings, girl.

 Jul. And joy comes well in such a needy time.
What are they, I beseech your ladyship?

 Lady. Well, well, thou hast a careful father, child;
One who, to put thee from thy heaviness,
Hath sorted out a sudden day of joy
That thou expects not nor I look'd not for.

 Jul. Madam, in happy time! What day is that?

 Lady. Marry, my child, early next Thursday morn
The gallant, young, and noble gentleman,
The County Paris, at Saint Peter's Church,
Shall happily make thee there a joyful bride.

 Jul. Now by Saint Peter's Church, and Peter too,
He shall not make me there a joyful bride!
I wonder at this haste, that I must wed
Ere he that should be husband comes to woo.
I pray you tell my lord and father, madam,
I will not marry yet; and when I do, I swear
It shall be Romeo, whom you know I hate,
Rather than Paris. These are news indeed!

Lady. Here comes your father. Tell him so yourself,
And see how be will take it at your hands.

Enter Capulet and Nurse.

Cap. When the sun sets the air doth drizzle dew,
But for the sunset of my brother's son
It rains downright.
How now? a conduit, girl? What, still in tears?
Evermore show'ring? In one little body
Thou counterfeit'st a bark, a sea, a wind:
For still thy eyes, which I may call the sea,
Do ebb and flow with tears; the bark thy body is
Sailing in this salt flood; the winds, thy sighs,
Who, raging with thy tears and they with them,
Without a sudden calm will overset
Thy tempest-tossed body. How now, wife?
Have you delivered to her our decree?

Lady. Ay, sir; but she will none, she gives you thanks.
I would the fool were married to her grave!

Cap. Soft! take me with you, take me with you, wife.
How? Will she none? Doth she not give us thanks?
Is she not proud? Doth she not count her blest,
Unworthy as she is, that we have wrought
So worthy a gentleman to be her bridegroom?

Jul. Not proud you have, but thankful that you have.
Proud can I never be of what I hate,
But thankful even for hate that is meant love.

Cap. How, how, how, how, choplogic? What is this?
'Proud'- and 'I thank you'- and 'I thank you not'-
And yet 'not proud'? Mistress minion you,
Thank me no thankings, nor proud me no prouds,
But fettle your fine joints 'gainst Thursday next
To go with Paris to Saint Peter's Church,
Or I will drag thee on a hurdle thither.
Out, you green-sickness carrion I out, you baggage!
You tallow-face!

Lady. Fie, fie! what, are you mad?

Jul. Good father, I beseech you on my knees,
Hear me with patience but to speak a word.

Cap. Hang thee, young baggage! disobedient wretch!
I tell thee what- get thee to church a Thursday
Or never after look me in the face.
Speak not, reply not, do not answer me!
My fingers itch. Wife, we scarce thought us blest
That God had lent us but this only child;
But now I see this one is one too much,
And that we have a curse in having her.
Out on her, hilding!

Nurse. God in heaven bless her!
You are to blame, my lord, to rate her so.

Cap. And why, my Lady Wisdom? Hold your tongue,
Good Prudence. Smatter with your gossips, go!

Nurse. I speak no treason.

Cap. O, God-i-god-en!

Nurse. May not one speak?

Cap. Peace, you mumbling fool!
Utter your gravity o'er a gossip's bowl,
For here we need it not.

Lady. You are too hot.

Cap. God's bread I it makes me mad. Day, night, late, early,
At home, abroad, alone, in company,
Waking or sleeping, still my care hath been
To have her match'd; and having now provided
A gentleman of princely parentage,
Of fair demesnes, youthful, and nobly train'd,
Stuff'd, as they say, with honourable parts,
Proportion'd as one's thought would wish a man-
And then to have a wretched puling fool,
A whining mammet, in her fortune's tender,
To answer 'I'll not wed, I cannot love;
I am too young, I pray you pardon me'!
But, an you will not wed, I'll pardon you.
Graze where you will, you shall not house with me.
Look to't, think on't; I do not use to jest.
Thursday is near; lay hand on heart, advise:
An you be mine, I'll give you to my friend;
An you be not, hang, beg, starve, die in the streets,
For, by my soul, I'll ne'er acknowledge thee,
Nor what is mine shall never do thee good.
Trust to't. Bethink you. I'll not be forsworn. Exit.

Jul. Is there no pity sitting in the clouds
That sees into the bottom of my grief?

O sweet my mother, cast me not away!
Delay this marriage for a month, a week;
Or if you do not, make the bridal bed
In that dim monument where Tybalt lies.

Lady. Talk not to me, for I'll not speak a word.
Do as thou wilt, for I have done with thee. Exit.

Jul. O God!- O nurse, how shall this be prevented?
My husband is on earth, my faith in heaven.
How shall that faith return again to earth
Unless that husband send it me from heaven
By leaving earth? Comfort me, counsel me.
Alack, alack, that heaven should practise stratagems
Upon so soft a subject as myself!
What say'st thou? Hast thou not a word of joy?
Some comfort, nurse.

Nurse. Faith, here it is.
Romeo is banish'd; and all the world to nothing
That he dares ne'er come back to challenge you;
Or if he do, it needs must be by stealth.
Then, since the case so stands as now it doth,
I think it best you married with the County.
O, he's a lovely gentleman!
Romeo's a dishclout to him. An eagle, madam,
Hath not so green, so quick, so fair an eye
As Paris hath. Beshrew my very heart,
I think you are happy in this second match,
For it excels your first; or if it did not,
Your first is dead- or 'twere as good he were
As living here and you no use of him.

Jul. Speak'st thou this from thy heart?

Nurse. And from my soul too; else beshrew them both.

Jul. Amen!

Nurse. What?

Jul. Well, thou hast comforted me marvellous much.
Go in; and tell my lady I am gone,
Having displeas'd my father, to Laurence' cell,
To make confession and to be absolv'd.

Nurse. Marry, I will; and this is wisely done. Exit.

Jul. Ancient damnation! O most wicked fiend!
Is it more sin to wish me thus forsworn,
Or to dispraise my lord with that same tongue
Which she hath prais'd him with above compare
So many thousand times? Go, counsellor!
Thou and my bosom henceforth shall be twain.
I'll to the friar to know his remedy.
If all else fail, myself have power to die. Exit.

Act Three, Scene Five Summary

The following morning, Romeo and Juliet lie in her bed, imagining the night has not really passed. The Nurse shows up with news that Juliet's mom is drawing nearer, so Romeo dives from the overhang and bids farewell.

Woman Capulet enlightens Juliet concerning the designs for her marriage, trusting it will perk her little girl up. Nonetheless, Juliet cannot, demanding she would prefer to wed Romeo Montague than wed Paris. (Clearly, her mom thinks this just an explanatory proclamation, since Romeo is Tybalt's killer.)

At that point, Lord Capulet enters, and becomes enraged at her refusal. He calls Juliet "youthful stuff," and requests she plan for marriage on the up and coming Thursday (3.5.160).

Woman Capulet won't intervene for Juliet, and even the Nurse double-crosses her, demanding that Paris is a fine man of his word deserving of her hand. Juliet orders the Nurse to leave, and plans to visit Friar Laurence for exhortation. As the Nurse leaves, Juliet calls her, "Antiquated punishment!" (3.5.235).

Act 3, Analysis

One of the most remarkable characteristics of Romeo and Juliet is the complex variety inside the play. A few researchers scrutinize the play as lopsided, while others acclaim Shakespeare's eagerness to investigate both appalling and comedic shows. In Act III, the play's tone moves from the generally funny sentiment of the initial two acts. Mercutio's passing makes unfavorable obstructions for Romeo and Juliet's all around laid plans, and discredits the probability of any evident harmony between the Montagues and Capulets.

Harold Bloom considers Mercutio one of the play's generally expressive and interesting characters. Mercutio gives a great part of the play's initial funniness through his articulated mind and sharp criticism. Be that as it may, in Act 3, his vitality takes a darker turn, as he shouts out "A plague o' both your homes" (3.1.101). The genuine loathsomeness of the quarrel is show in the manner Mercutio utilizes his withering breaths to shout this expression multiple times - making it sound like a real revile. Furthermore, Mercutio's demise powers Romeo's progress from adolescence into adulthood. Though previously, Romeo had the option to isolate himself from his family's resentment, his choice to vindicate Mercutio's demise by executing Tybalt rather energizes the quarrel he had once would have liked to get away.

The Nurse's first appearance Act 3 strengthens the move to catastrophe. Her powerlessness (or refusal) to practically impart her news to Juilet echoes the prior scene (II.iv), when she prodded Juliet. In any case, while that scene was played for satire, a similar gadget gets maddening and barbarous under the disastrous conditions. These equal scenes set up the tonal move of the play. As a side note, the equal additionally uncovers the complexities of the Nurse's character. Despite the fact that Shakespeare could have kept in touch with her as just a practical character, he rather gives her layers - she is characterized by her support of a young lady whom she additionally hates.

The repetitive uniqueness among request and confusion additionally returns in Act 3. Juliet conveys one of the play's most lovely discourses, when she asks for sunset - which Shakespeare has built up as a period of request and security. Juliet says, "Come, delicate night; come, cherishing, dark browed night,/Give me my Romeo, and when he will bite the dust/Take him and cut him out in little stars,/And he will make the essence of paradise so fine/That all the world will be infatuated with night/And pay no love to the pompous sun" (3.2.20-25). The emotional incongruity of her discourse – the crowd knows now that Romeo has executed Tybalt and will before long be rebuffed, while Juliet doesn't – just underscores the power of the partition among request and turmoil now. Each outstanding scene set in obscurity – the room and afterward the vault – will be set apart by the characters' shocking mindfulness that once the sun rises, they will be dependent upon mayhem and torment.

The contention that that Romeo and Juliet is definitely not an old style disaster increases some assurance with the conditions encompassing the horrible occasions that happen in Act 3. In spite of the fact that Mercutio and Tybalt's demises and Romeo's expulsion are without a doubt lamentable, they are avoidable events as opposed to being commanded by destiny - which would be the situation in an old style catastrophe. Rather, these passings are the aftereffect of an avoidable quarrel. The double mortalities happen after the characters arbitrarily run into one another in the city, yet the gore is empowered by explicit human choices. Romeo decides to seek after retribution on Tybalt, not for a minute thinking about how his activities will influence his new spouse. The genuinely charged conditions, however unfortunate, present a decision, not a certainty. Particularly thinking about how Romeo has maintained a strategic distance from savagery and hostility thusfar in the play, it is anything but difficult to contend that he is to a great extent to fault for the play's shocking turn.

Then again, one could contend that the terrible powers at work are relentless despite the fact that they are man-made. The quarrel between the Montagues and the Capulets is more impressive than the affection among Romeo and Juliet - and in this way, it inevitably overcomes them. Romeo initially has little enthusiasm for including himself in his family's undertakings, however Mercutio's passing straightforwardly influences him. Further, one could contend that the "plague" Mercutio puts on the houses is the purpose behind the darlings' demises. In the last demonstration of Romeo and Juliet, Friar John discloses his failure to convey the letter to Romeo: "the searchers of the town,/Suspecting that we both were in a house/Where the irresistible epidemic reigned,/Sealed up the entryways, and would not let us forward" (5.2.8-11). The way that a genuine "plague" rerouted the letter proposes that more noteworthy powers had a job in the appalling completion.

Notwithstanding old style shows, Shakespeare leaves little uncertainty over his awful expectations through the play's attention on death. For example, he presents the picture of the wheel of fortune in Act 1 when the Nurse talks about how Juliet has developed from a modest little girl into a tough lady, while in Act 3, she reveals to Romeo that the young lady "destructions once more" (3.3.101). Afterward, Juliet takes this picture considerably further, saying, "Methinks I see thee, presently thou workmanship so low/As one dead in the base of a tomb" (3.5.55-6). Juliet's character bend follows her developing trust in the early demonstrations, however rapidly drops into disaster as the play reaches a conclusion. Besides, Shakespeare by and by utilizes the picture of death as Juliet's groom. Woman Capulet remarks about Juliet's refusal to wed Paris: "I would the imbecile were hitched to her grave" (3.5.140). This expression works out as expected, in light of the fact that Juliet bites the dust while she is as yet hitched to Romeo.

The exceptional love among Romeo and Juliet, in any case, is a contradiction to the disaster that whirls around them. In Act 3, the sweethearts anticipate culminating their relationship. In any case, sex, a channel to new life, shockingly denotes the start of the succession that will end in Romeo and Juliet's demises. In Act 3, Shakespeare keeps on characterizing love as a condition wherein darlings can investigate benevolent dedication by the egotistical demonstration of withdrawing into a private case. For example, Juliet's commitment to her marriage is solid all through the Act. Despite the fact that she at first ridicules Romeo for executing Tybalt, she rapidly adjusts herself, soliciting, "Will I tear down him that is my significant other?" (3.2.97). She relentlessly demands that she would forfeit ten thousand Tybalts and her own folks to be with Romeo. While Juliet's decree fortifies the profundity of her adoration, it additionally reminds the crowd that genuine affection exists in private domain, isolated from moral codes and desires.

Romeo likewise exhibits the profundity of his pledge to his cherished, however not with a similar assurance as his significant other. Though Juliet gets quality from her despondency, Romeo quickly surrenders to wretchedness. He broadcasts, "At that point 'expelled'/is passing mistermed. Calling demise 'expelled'/Thou cut's my head off with a brilliant hatchet" (3.3.20-22). Both Friar Laurence and the Nurse scold Romeo his negativity, since he and Juliet are both still alive – yet his solipsism is with the end goal that he comes up short on any more extensive point of view.

Shakespeare subverts sexual orientation jobs again by having Juliet show a more unemotional determination than her significant other. At the point when the Nurse demands that Romeo "stand, a you take care of business," she is verifiably proposing that he has been acting in a ladylike way (III.iii.88). Shakespeare additionally helps the crowd to remember the current man controlled society through Lord Capulet, who sees Juliet just as an article to be traded. Despite the fact that Capulet at first professes to have his little girl's government assistance at the top of the priority list, he rapidly turns merciless when she opposes him. Juliet's quality is praiseworthy to the crowd, yet is utter horror to men, similar to her dad, whose power she is compromising.

The contention among Juliet and her dad is another case of the divergence among youthful and old, which seems a few times in Act 3. Romeo discusses Friar Laurence's numbness of his affection for Juliet, saying that the Friar would never comprehend on the grounds that he isn't "youthful." Furthermore, the last scene uncovers how grown-ups cannot, at this point comprehend energetic energy. Woman Capulet will not think about Juliet's refusal to wed Paris, and even the Nurse discusses Paris as a prudent man deserving of her hand (consequently uncovering her hidden disdain of her young charge). In light of the Nurse's disparaging depiction of Paris, Juliet yells, "Old perdition!" (3.5.235). This fills in as both reference to the Nurse's age and to the issues she should manage, all of which have been made by a fight that has its underlying foundations in the more seasoned age. Romeo and Juliet are two youngsters, who have fallen inevitably enamored - just to bang into the political ruses of their older folks - a pickle that has resounded sincerely with adolescents for ages.

ACT IV. Scene I. Friar Laurence's cell.

Enter Friar, [Laurence] and County Paris.

Friar. On Thursday, sir? The time is very short.

  Par. My father Capulet will have it so,
  And I am nothing slow to slack his haste.

  Friar. You say you do not know the lady's mind.
  Uneven is the course; I like it not.

  Par. Immoderately she weeps for Tybalt's death,
  And therefore have I little talk'd of love;
  For Venus smiles not in a house of tears.
  Now, sir, her father counts it dangerous
  That she do give her sorrow so much sway,
  And in his wisdom hastes our marriage
  To stop the inundation of her tears,
  Which, too much minded by herself alone,
  May be put from her by society.
  Now do you know the reason of this haste.

  Friar. [aside] I would I knew not why it should be slow'd.-
  Look, sir, here comes the lady toward my cell.

Enter Juliet.

Par. Happily met, my lady and my wife!

Jul. That may be, sir, when I may be a wife.

Par. That may be must be, love, on Thursday next.

Jul. What must be shall be.

Friar. That's a certain text.

Par. Come you to make confession to this father?

Jul. To answer that, I should confess to you.

Par. Do not deny to him that you love me.

Jul. I will confess to you that I love him.

Par. So will ye, I am sure, that you love me.

  Jul. If I do so, it will be of more price,
    Being spoke behind your back, than to your face.

Par. Poor soul, thy face is much abus'd with tears.

  Jul. The tears have got small victory by that,
    For it was bad enough before their spite.

Par. Thou wrong'st it more than tears with that report.

  Jul. That is no slander, sir, which is a truth;
    And what I spake, I spake it to my face.

Par. Thy face is mine, and thou hast sland'red it.

  Jul. It may be so, for it is not mine own.
    Are you at leisure, holy father, now,
    Or shall I come to you at evening mass

  Friar. My leisure serves me, pensive daughter, now.
    My lord, we must entreat the time alone.

Par. God shield I should disturb devotion!
Juliet, on Thursday early will I rouse ye.
Till then, adieu, and keep this holy kiss.   Exit.

Jul. O, shut the door! and when thou hast done so,
Come weep with me- past hope, past cure, past help!

Friar. Ah, Juliet, I already know thy grief;
It strains me past the compass of my wits.
I hear thou must, and nothing may prorogue it,
On Thursday next be married to this County.

Jul. Tell me not, friar, that thou hear'st of this,
Unless thou tell me how I may prevent it.
If in thy wisdom thou canst give no help,
Do thou but call my resolution wise
And with this knife I'll help it presently.
God join'd my heart and Romeo's, thou our hands;
And ere this hand, by thee to Romeo's seal'd,
Shall be the label to another deed,
Or my true heart with treacherous revolt
Turn to another, this shall slay them both.
Therefore, out of thy long-experienc'd time,
Give me some present counsel; or, behold,
'Twixt my extremes and me this bloody knife
Shall play the empire, arbitrating that
Which the commission of thy years and art
Could to no issue of true honour bring.
Be not so long to speak. I long to die
If what thou speak'st speak not of remedy.

Friar. Hold, daughter. I do spy a kind of hope,
Which craves as desperate an execution

As that is desperate which we would prevent.
If, rather than to marry County Paris
Thou hast the strength of will to slay thyself,
Then is it likely thou wilt undertake
A thing like death to chide away this shame,
That cop'st with death himself to scape from it;
And, if thou dar'st, I'll give thee remedy.

Jul. O, bid me leap, rather than marry Paris,
From off the battlements of yonder tower,
Or walk in thievish ways, or bid me lurk
Where serpents are; chain me with roaring bears,
Or shut me nightly in a charnel house,
O'ercover'd quite with dead men's rattling bones,
With reeky shanks and yellow chapless skulls;
Or bid me go into a new-made grave
And hide me with a dead man in his shroud-
Things that, to hear them told, have made me tremble-
And I will do it without fear or doubt,
To live an unstain'd wife to my sweet love.

Friar. Hold, then. Go home, be merry, give consent
To marry Paris. Wednesday is to-morrow.
To-morrow night look that thou lie alone;
Let not the nurse lie with thee in thy chamber.
Take thou this vial, being then in bed,
And this distilled liquor drink thou off;
When presently through all thy veins shall run
A cold and drowsy humour; for no pulse
Shall keep his native progress, but surcease;
No warmth, no breath, shall testify thou livest;
The roses in thy lips and cheeks shall fade
To paly ashes, thy eyes' windows fall

Like death when he shuts up the day of life;
Each part, depriv'd of supple government,
Shall, stiff and stark and cold, appear like death;
And in this borrowed likeness of shrunk death
Thou shalt continue two-and-forty hours,
And then awake as from a pleasant sleep.
Now, when the bridegroom in the morning comes
To rouse thee from thy bed, there art thou dead.
Then, as the manner of our country is,
In thy best robes uncovered on the bier
Thou shalt be borne to that same ancient vault
Where all the kindred of the Capulets lie.
In the mean time, against thou shalt awake,
Shall Romeo by my letters know our drift;
And hither shall he come; and he and I
Will watch thy waking, and that very night
Shall Romeo bear thee hence to Mantua.
And this shall free thee from this present shame,
If no inconstant toy nor womanish fear
Abate thy valour in the acting it.

Jul. Give me, give me! O, tell not me of fear!

Friar. Hold! Get you gone, be strong and prosperous
In this resolve. I'll send a friar with speed
To Mantua, with my letters to thy lord.

Jul. Love give me strength! and strength shall help afford.
Farewell, dear father.
        Exeunt.

Act Four, Scene One Summary

At the church, Paris addresses Friar Laurence about his looming wedding to Juliet. Mindful of the complexities that will emerge from this new match, the Friar is loaded with hesitations.

Juliet, looking for Romeo, shows up at the house of prayer and discovers Paris there. She is compelled to talk with him, and he carries on haughtily since their wedding is set. In any case, Juliet repels him with her obscure answers, and afterward at last inquires as to whether she may address only him. At the point when the Friar consents, Paris is driven out.

Monk Laurence proposes a confused arrangement to help Juliet rejoin with Romeo. The Friar will give Juliet an exceptional elixir that will viably kill her for 48 hours; she will show no indications of life. Following their family custom, her folks will put her body in the Capulet vault. In the mean time, Friar Laurence will send a letter to Romeo, educating him of the arrangement so the kid can meet Juliet in the tomb and afterward lead her away from Verona. Juliet affirms of the arrangement.

Scene II. Capulet's house.

Enter Father Capulet, Mother, Nurse, and Servingmen, two or three.

Cap. So many guests invite as here are writ.
[Exit a Servingman.]
Sirrah, go hire me twenty cunning cooks.

Serv. You shall have none ill, sir; for I'll try if they can lick their fingers.

Cap. How canst thou try them so?

Serv. Marry, sir, 'tis an ill cook that cannot lick his own fingers. Therefore he that cannot lick his fingers goes not
  with me.

Cap. Go, begone.
                      Exit Servingman.
We shall be much unfurnish'd for this time.
What, is my daughter gone to Friar Laurence?

Nurse. Ay, forsooth.

Cap. Well, be may chance to do some good on her.
A peevish self-will'd harlotry it is.

Enter Juliet.

Nurse. See where she comes from shrift with merry look.

Cap. How now, my headstrong? Where have you been gadding?

Jul. Where I have learnt me to repent the sin
  Of disobedient opposition
  To you and your behests, and am enjoin'd
  By holy Laurence to fall prostrate here
  To beg your pardon. Pardon, I beseech you!
  Henceforward I am ever rul'd by you.

Cap. Send for the County. Go tell him of this.
I'll have this knot knit up to-morrow morning.

Jul. I met the youthful lord at Laurence' cell
And gave him what becomed love I might,
Not stepping o'er the bounds of modesty.

Cap. Why, I am glad on't. This is well. Stand up.
This is as't should be. Let me see the County.
Ay, marry, go, I say, and fetch him hither.
Now, afore God, this reverend holy friar,
All our whole city is much bound to him.

Jul. Nurse, will you go with me into my closet
To help me sort such needful ornaments
As you think fit to furnish me to-morrow?

Mother. No, not till Thursday. There is time enough.

Cap. Go, nurse, go with her. We'll to church to-morrow.
                Exeunt Juliet and Nurse.

Mother. We shall be short in our provision.
'Tis now near night.

Cap. Tush, I will stir about,
And all things shall be well, I warrant thee, wife.
Go thou to Juliet, help to deck up her.
I'll not to bed to-night; let me alone.
I'll play the housewife for this once. What, ho!
They are all forth; well, I will walk myself
To County Paris, to prepare him up

Against to-morrow. My heart is wondrous light,
Since this same wayward girl is so reclaim'd.
Exeunt.

Act Four, Scene Two Summary

Glad to realize that she will be brought together with Romeo, Juliet gets back and apologizes to her dad for her noncompliance. He acquits her, and trains her to set up her garments for the wedding, which is currently going to happen the following day. Master Capulet then embarks to discover Paris to convey the uplifting news about Juliet's difference in heart.

Scene III. Juliet's chamber.

Enter Juliet and Nurse.

Jul. Ay, those attires are best; but, gentle nurse,
I pray thee leave me to myself to-night;
For I have need of many orisons
To move the heavens to smile upon my state,
Which, well thou knowest, is cross and full of sin.

Enter Mother.

Mother. What, are you busy, ho? Need you my help?

Jul. No, madam; we have cull'd such necessaries
As are behooffull for our state to-morrow.
So please you, let me now be left alone,
And let the nurse this night sit up with you;
For I am sure you have your hands full all
In this so sudden business.

Mother. Good night.
Get thee to bed, and rest; for thou hast need.
                       Exeunt [Mother and Nurse.]

Jul. Farewell! God knows when we shall meet again.
I have a faint cold fear thrills through my veins
That almost freezes up the heat of life.
I'll call them back again to comfort me.
Nurse!- What should she do here?
My dismal scene I needs must act alone.
Come, vial.
What if this mixture do not work at all?
Shall I be married then to-morrow morning?
No, No! This shall forbid it. Lie thou there.
                       Lays down a dagger.
What if it be a poison which the friar
Subtilly hath minist'red to have me dead,
Lest in this marriage he should be dishonour'd
Because he married me before to Romeo?
I fear it is; and yet methinks it should not,
For he hath still been tried a holy man.
I will not entertain so bad a thought.
How if, when I am laid into the tomb,
I wake before the time that Romeo
Come to redeem me? There's a fearful point!
Shall I not then be stifled in the vault,
To whose foul mouth no healthsome air breathes in,
And there die strangled ere my Romeo comes?
Or, if I live, is it not very like
The horrible conceit of death and night,
Together with the terror of the place-
As in a vault, an ancient receptacle
Where for this many hundred years the bones
Of all my buried ancestors are pack'd;
Where bloody Tybalt, yet but green in earth,

Lies fest'ring in his shroud; where, as they say,
At some hours in the night spirits resort-
Alack, alack, is it not like that I,
So early waking- what with loathsome smells,
And shrieks like mandrakes torn out of the earth,
That living mortals, hearing them, run mad-
O, if I wake, shall I not be distraught,
Environed with all these hideous fears,
And madly play with my forefathers' joints,
And pluck the mangled Tybalt from his shroud.,
And, in this rage, with some great kinsman's bone
As with a club dash out my desp'rate brains?
O, look! methinks I see my cousin's ghost
Seeking out Romeo, that did spit his body
Upon a rapier's point. Stay, Tybalt, stay!
Romeo, I come! this do I drink to thee.

She [drinks and] falls upon her bed within the curtains.

Act Four, Scene Three Summary

Juliet persuades Lady Capulet and the Nurse to leave her rest be that night. Juliet keeps a blade close by in the event that the elixir ought to fizzle. She at that point drinks the Friar's mixture and tumbles to her bed, unmoving.

Scene IV. Capulet's house.

Enter Lady of the House and Nurse.

Lady. Hold, take these keys and fetch more spices, nurse.

Nurse. They call for dates and quinces in the pastry.

Enter Old Capulet.

Cap. Come, stir, stir, stir! The second cock hath crow'd,
The curfew bell hath rung, 'tis three o'clock.
Look to the bak'd meats, good Angelica;
Spare not for cost.

Nurse. Go, you cot-quean, go,
Get you to bed! Faith, you'll be sick to-morrow
For this night's watching.

Cap. No, not a whit. What, I have watch'd ere now
All night for lesser cause, and ne'er been sick.

Lady. Ay, you have been a mouse-hunt in your time;
But I will watch you from such watching now.
                    Exeunt Lady and Nurse.

Cap. A jealous hood, a jealous hood!

Enter three or four [Fellows, with spits and logs and baskets.

What is there? Now, fellow,

Fellow. Things for the cook, sir; but I know not what.

  Cap. Make haste, make haste. [Exit Fellow.] Sirrah, fetch drier
     logs.
  Call Peter; he will show thee where they are.

Fellow. I have a head, sir, that will find out logs
  And never trouble Peter for the matter.

  Cap. Mass, and well said; a merry whoreson, ha!
   Thou shalt be loggerhead. [Exit Fellow.] Good faith,
'tis day.
   The County will be here with music straight,
   For so he said he would. Play music.
   I hear him near.
   Nurse! Wife! What, ho! What, nurse, I say!

                Enter Nurse.
   Go waken Juliet; go and trim her up.
   I'll go and chat with Paris. Hie, make haste,
   Make haste! The bridegroom he is come already:
   Make haste, I say.
                        [Exeunt.]

Scene V. Juliet's chamber.

[Enter Nurse.]

  Nurse. Mistress! what, mistress! Juliet! Fast, I warrant
her, she.
   Why, lamb! why, lady! Fie, you slug-abed!
   Why, love, I say! madam! sweetheart! Why, bride!
   What, not a word? You take your pennyworths now!
   Sleep for a week; for the next night, I warrant,
   The County Paris hath set up his rest
   That you shall rest but little. God forgive me!
   Marry, and amen. How sound is she asleep!
   I needs must wake her. Madam, madam, madam!

Ay, let the County take you in your bed!
He'll fright you up, i' faith. Will it not be?
             [Draws aside the curtains.]
What, dress'd, and in your clothes, and down again?
I must needs wake you. Lady! lady! lady!
Alas, alas! Help, help! My lady's dead!
O weraday that ever I was born!
Some aqua-vitae, ho! My lord! my lady!

Enter Mother.

Mother. What noise is here?

Nurse. O lamentable day!

Mother. What is the matter?

Nurse. Look, look! O heavy day!

  Mother. O me, O me! My child, my only life!
    Revive, look up, or I will die with thee!
    Help, help! Call help.

Enter Father.

Father. For shame, bring Juliet forth; her lord is come.

Nurse. She's dead, deceas'd; she's dead! Alack the day!

Mother. Alack the day, she's dead, she's dead, she's dead!

  Cap. Ha! let me see her. Out alas! she's cold,
    Her blood is settled, and her joints are stiff;
    Life and these lips have long been separated.
    Death lies on her like an untimely frost

Upon the sweetest flower of all the field.

Nurse. O lamentable day!

Mother. O woful time!

Cap. Death, that hath ta'en her hence to make me wail,
Ties up my tongue and will not let me speak.

Enter Friar [Laurence] and the County [Paris], with Musicians.

Friar. Come, is the bride ready to go to church?

Cap. Ready to go, but never to return.
O son, the night before thy wedding day
Hath Death lain with thy wife. See, there she lies,
Flower as she was, deflowered by him.
Death is my son-in-law, Death is my heir;
My daughter he hath wedded. I will die
And leave him all. Life, living, all is Death's.

Par. Have I thought long to see this morning's face,
And doth it give me such a sight as this?

Mother. Accurs'd, unhappy, wretched, hateful day!
Most miserable hour that e'er time saw
In lasting labour of his pilgrimage!
But one, poor one, one poor and loving child,
But one thing to rejoice and solace in,
And cruel Death hath catch'd it from my sight!

Nurse. O woe? O woful, woful, woful day!
Most lamentable day, most woful day

That ever ever I did yet behold!
O day! O day! O day! O hateful day!
Never was seen so black a day as this.
O woful day! O woful day!

Par. Beguil'd, divorced, wronged, spited, slain!
Most detestable Death, by thee beguil'd,
By cruel cruel thee quite overthrown!
O love! O life! not life, but love in death

Cap. Despis'd, distressed, hated, martyr'd, kill'd!
Uncomfortable time, why cam'st thou now
To murther, murther our solemnity?
O child! O child! my soul, and not my child!
Dead art thou, dead! alack, my child is dead,
And with my child my joys are buried!

Friar. Peace, ho, for shame! Confusion's cure lives not
In these confusions. Heaven and yourself
Had part in this fair maid! now heaven hath all,
And all the better is it for the maid.
Your part in her you could not keep from death,
But heaven keeps his part in eternal life.
The most you sought was her promotion,
For 'twas your heaven she should be advanc'd;
And weep ye now, seeing she is advanc'd
Above the clouds, as high as heaven itself?
O, in this love, you love your child so ill
That you run mad, seeing that she is well.
She's not well married that lives married long,
But she's best married that dies married young.
Dry up your tears and stick your rosemary
On this fair corse, and, as the custom is,

In all her best array bear her to church;
For though fond nature bids us all lament,
Yet nature's tears are reason's merriment.

Cap. All things that we ordained festival
Turn from their office to black funeral-
Our instruments to melancholy bells,
Our wedding cheer to a sad burial feast;
Our solemn hymns to sullen dirges change;
Our bridal flowers serve for a buried corse;
And all things change them to the contrary.

Friar. Sir, go you in; and, madam, go with him;
And go, Sir Paris. Every one prepare
To follow this fair corse unto her grave.
The heavens do low'r upon you for some ill;
Move them no more by crossing their high will.
    Exeunt. Manent Musicians [and Nurse].
1. Mus. Faith, we may put up our pipes and be gone.

Nurse. Honest good fellows, ah, put up, put up!
 For well you know this is a pitiful case. [Exit.]
1. Mus. Ay, by my troth, the case may be amended.

Enter Peter.

Pet. Musicians, O, musicians, 'Heart's ease,' 'Heart's ease'!
 O, an you will have me live, play 'Heart's ease.'
1. Mus. Why 'Heart's ease'',

Pet. O, musicians, because my heart itself plays 'My heart is
  full of woe.' O, play me some merry dump to comfort me.
1. Mus. Not a dump we! 'Tis no time to play now.

Pet. You will not then?
1. Mus. No.

Pet. I will then give it you soundly.
1. Mus. What will you give us?

Pet. No money, on my faith, but the gleek. I will give you the
  minstrel.
1. Mus. Then will I give you the serving-creature.

Pet. Then will I lay the serving-creature's dagger on your pate.
  I will carry no crotchets. I'll re you, I'll fa you. Do you note me?
1. Mus. An you re us and fa us, you note us.
2. Mus. Pray you put up your dagger, and put out your wit.

Pet. Then have at you with my wit! I will dry-beat you with an
  iron wit, and put up my iron dagger. Answer me like men.

'When griping grief the heart doth wound,
   And doleful dumps the mind oppress,
  Then music with her silver sound'-

  Why 'silver sound'? Why 'music with her silver sound'?
  What say you, Simon Catling?
 1. Mus. Marry, sir, because silver hath a sweet sound.

  Pet. Pretty! What say You, Hugh Rebeck?
  2. Mus. I say 'silver sound' because musicians sound for silver.

  Pet. Pretty too! What say you, James Soundpost?
  3. Mus. Faith, I know not what to say.

  Pet. O, I cry you mercy! you are the singer. I will say for you. It
   is 'music with her silver sound' because musicians have no
    gold for sounding.

   'Then music with her silver sound
     With speedy help doth lend redress.' [Exit.

  1. Mus. What a pestilent knave is this same?
  2. Mus. Hang him, Jack! Come, we'll in here, tarry for the
    mourners, and stay dinner.
                               Exeunt.

Act Four, Scene Four & 5 Summary

At the point when the Nurse shows up to bring Juliet the following morning, she finds the little youngster's dormant body. Woman Capulet before long follows, and is justifiably crushed over her girl's clear suicide. At the point when Lord Capulet discovers his girl is dead, he arranges the wedding music to move into memorial service laments. The lamenting family gets ready to move Juliet's body to the Capulet tomb as quickly as time permits.

Act 4, Analysis

As noted in the past Analysis segments, Shakespeare anticipates Romeo and Juliet's disastrous consummation by peppering the entire play with pictures of death. In Act 4, demise at long last goes to the cutting edge. Despite the fact that the crowd comprehends that Juliet's passing is a ploy, watching her arrangement and execute her suicide is an enthusiastic minute - the extraordinary measures Juliet and Romeo are happy to take to be as one are evidence of their deplorable edginess.

In Act 4, Juliet brings every last bit of her interior quality, which is show in her readiness to take part in the Friar's rash and shaky arrangement. Romeo doesn't show up right now; causes it to feel like Shakespeare needed to cause to notice Juliet's faithful commitment towards taking care of their concern. Where Romeo's responded to his expulsion by really endeavoring suicide in Act 3, Juliet takes a gander at the issue sensibly, deciding to pretend suicide so as to rejoin with her sweetheart. These equal choices recommend Juliet's predominant boldness and shrewdness, and demonstrate the intensity of affection in Romeo and Juliet.

Juliet's activities underline the common division between the youthful and the old in the play. Her choice to conform to the Friar's arrangement may be imprudent, however it is certainly daring. Then again, the grown-ups in Act 4 act solely out of acquiescence and personal responsibility. Paris is done attempting to beguile or charm Juliet however, after hearing the news that she has acknowledged his hand, gets self-important and repulsive. Juliet's folks no longer fret about her prosperity once she professes to acknowledge her prearranged engagement to Paris, and even the Nurse (who knows the profundity of her energy for Romeo) permits her to rest alone. Just the youthful sweethearts know the triumph and the catastrophe of genuine romance, while their more established partners unemotionally acknowledge the state of affairs, preferring simplicity and convenience. Juliet's folks are glad to the point that she has consented to the beneficial match with Paris that they never question why she has adjusted her perspective on him so rapidly.

From the earliest starting point of Romeo and Juliet, Friar Laurence appears to be more similar to a government official than a blessed man. He realizes that Romeo and Juliet's marriage is hurried and nonsensical yet considers it to be an approach to arrange harmony between the Montagues and the Capulets. In the principal scene of Act 4, Friar Laurence makes no endeavor to meddle with Paris' marriage plans, despite the fact that the Friar realizes that Juliet is now hitched. He comes up short on the boldness to express reality, despite the fact that he realizes that Juliet and Paris' marriage would be finished heresy. Moreover, the Friar permits Juliet to utilize the holy observance of repentance to dispose of Paris, which is another case of his disregard for strict shows. At last, the Friar's silly arrangement causes him to appear to be more similar to a crazy lab rat than a cleric. He could have helped Romeo and Juliet to just flee, yet had he done as such, he would have lost a chance to accommodate the quarrel between the Montagues and Capulets. By designing a bogus catastrophe and playing with death, Friar Laurence uncovers his needs - his own longing for political impact is a higher priority than the sweethearts' joy or his own strict pledges.

At long last, the Friar's tangled arrangement calls the play's unfortunate classification into further inquiry. While the consummation of Romeo and Juliet is obviously dismal, it gets moving further far from the tropes of traditional catastrophe. The way that Juliet concurs the Friar's wild arrangement rather than essentially fleeing (which is a sensible choice, particularly since Romeo has just been expelled) proposes that the characters' decisions assume a significant job in the darlings' definitive death. In a traditional disaster, destiny and other undaunted powers lead to cataclysmic occasions. Nonetheless, in the Friar and Juliet's arrangement, it appears that Juliet can't completely give up her life in Verona – she needs to guarantee triumph over her folks. She is too obstinate to even think about wondering whether her energetic bluster may have its own negative results.

ACT V. Scene I. Mantua. A street.

Enter Romeo.

  Rom. If I may trust the flattering truth of sleep
    My dreams presage some joyful news at hand.
    My bosom's lord sits lightly in his throne,
    And all this day an unaccustom'd spirit
    Lifts me above the ground with cheerful thoughts.
    I dreamt my lady came and found me dead
    (Strange dream that gives a dead man leave to think!)
    And breath'd such life with kisses in my lips
    That I reviv'd and was an emperor.
    Ah me! how sweet is love itself possess'd,
    When but love's shadows are so rich in joy!

Enter Romeo's Man Balthasar, booted.

    News from Verona! How now, Balthasar?
    Dost thou not bring me letters from the friar?
    How doth my lady? Is my father well?
    How fares my Juliet? That I ask again,
    For nothing can be ill if she be well.

  Man. Then she is well, and nothing can be ill.
    Her body sleeps in Capel's monument,
    And her immortal part with angels lives.
    I saw her laid low in her kindred's vault
    And presently took post to tell it you.
    O, pardon me for bringing these ill news,
    Since you did leave it for my office, sir.

  Rom. Is it e'en so? Then I defy you, stars!
    Thou knowest my lodging. Get me ink and paper

And hire posthorses. I will hence to-night.

Man. I do beseech you, sir, have patience.
Your looks are pale and wild and do import
Some misadventure.

Rom. Tush, thou art deceiv'd.
Leave me and do the thing I bid thee do.
Hast thou no letters to me from the friar?

Man. No, my good lord.

Rom. No matter. Get thee gone
And hire those horses. I'll be with thee straight.
       Exit [Balthasar].
Well, Juliet, I will lie with thee to-night.
Let's see for means. O mischief, thou art swift
To enter in the thoughts of desperate men!
I do remember an apothecary,
And hereabouts 'a dwells, which late I noted
In tatt'red weeds, with overwhelming brows,
Culling of simples. Meagre were his looks,
Sharp misery had worn him to the bones;
And in his needy shop a tortoise hung,
An alligator stuff'd, and other skins
Of ill-shaped fishes; and about his shelves
A beggarly account of empty boxes,
Green earthen pots, bladders, and musty seeds,
Remnants of packthread, and old cakes of roses
Were thinly scattered, to make up a show.
Noting this penury, to myself I said,
'An if a man did need a poison now
Whose sale is present death in Mantua,
Here lives a caitiff wretch would sell it him.'

O, this same thought did but forerun my need,
And this same needy man must sell it me.
As I remember, this should be the house.
Being holiday, the beggar's shop is shut. What, ho! apothecary!

Enter Apothecary.

Apoth. Who calls so loud?

Rom. Come hither, man. I see that thou art poor.
Hold, there is forty ducats. Let me have
A dram of poison, such soon-speeding gear
As will disperse itself through all the veins
That the life-weary taker mall fall dead,
And that the trunk may be discharg'd of breath
As violently as hasty powder fir'd
Doth hurry from the fatal cannon's womb.

Apoth. Such mortal drugs I have; but Mantua's law
Is death to any he that utters them.

Rom. Art thou so bare and full of wretchedness
And fearest to die? Famine is in thy cheeks,
Need and oppression starveth in thine eyes,
Contempt and beggary hangs upon thy back:
The world is not thy friend, nor the world's law;
The world affords no law to make thee rich;
Then be not poor, but break it and take this.

Apoth. My poverty but not my will consents.

Rom. I pay thy poverty and not thy will.

Apoth. Put this in any liquid thing you will
And drink it off, and if you had the strength
Of twenty men, it would dispatch you straight.

Rom. There is thy gold- worse poison to men's souls,
Doing more murther in this loathsome world,
Than these poor compounds that thou mayst not sell.
I sell thee poison; thou hast sold me none.
Farewell. Buy food and get thyself in flesh.
Come, cordial and not poison, go with me
To Juliet's grave; for there must I use thee.
                    Exeunt.

Act Five, Scene One Summary

Romeo meanders the boulevards of Mantua, thinking about a fantasy he had the prior night where Juliet was dead. At that point, Balthasar shows up from Verona with the updates on Juliet's clear suicide.

Romeo promptly arranges Balthasar to set up a pony so he can race to Verona and see Juliet's body. In the interim, he composes a letter for Balthasar to provide for Lord Montague, clarifying the circumstance. At last, before he leaves Mantua, Romeo gets some toxic substance from a poor Apothecary.

Scene II. Verona. Friar Laurence's cell.

Enter Friar John to Friar Laurence.

John. Holy Franciscan friar, brother, ho!

Enter Friar Laurence.

Laur. This same should be the voice of Friar John.
Welcome from Mantua. What says Romeo?
Or, if his mind be writ, give me his letter.

John. Going to find a barefoot brother out,
One of our order, to associate me
Here in this city visiting the sick,
And finding him, the searchers of the town,
Suspecting that we both were in a house
Where the infectious pestilence did reign,
Seal'd up the doors, and would not let us forth,
So that my speed to Mantua there was stay'd.

Laur. Who bare my letter, then, to Romeo?

John. I could not send it- here it is again-
Nor get a messenger to bring it thee,
So fearful were they of infection.

Laur. Unhappy fortune! By my brotherhood,
The letter was not nice, but full of charge,
Of dear import; and the neglecting it
May do much danger. Friar John, go hence,
Get me an iron crow and bring it straight
Unto my cell.

John. Brother, I'll go and bring it thee. Exit.

Laur. Now, must I to the monument alone.
Within this three hours will fair Juliet wake.
She will beshrew me much that Romeo
Hath had no notice of these accidents;
But I will write again to Mantua,

And keep her at my cell till Romeo come-
Poor living corse, clos'd in a dead man's tomb! Exit.

Act Five, Scene Two Summary

Back in Verona, Friar John, who should convey the letter to Romeo educating him concerning the arrangement, apologizes to Friar Laurence for his powerlessness to finish the undertaking. Evidently, during his excursion, a few people accepted that Friar John conveyed the disease (the plague) and secured him a house.

Minister Laurence understands this new wrinkle crashes his arrangement, so he quickly arranges a crowbar with the goal that he can save Juliet from the Capulet tomb.

Scene III. Verona. A churchyard; in it the monument of the Capulets.

Enter Paris and his Page with flowers and [a torch].

Par. Give me thy torch, boy. Hence, and stand aloof.
Yet put it out, for I would not be seen.
Under yond yew tree lay thee all along,
Holding thine ear close to the hollow ground.
So shall no foot upon the churchyard tread
(Being loose, unfirm, with digging up of graves)
But thou shalt hear it. Whistle then to me,
As signal that thou hear'st something approach.
Give me those flowers. Do as I bid thee, go.

Page. [aside] I am almost afraid to stand alone
  Here in the churchyard; yet I will adventure. [Retires.]

Par. Sweet flower, with flowers thy bridal bed I strew
  (O woe! thy canopy is dust and stones)
  Which with sweet water nightly I will dew;
  Or, wanting that, with tears distill'd by moans.
  The obsequies that I for thee will keep
  Nightly shall be to strew, thy grave and weep.
                    Whistle Boy.
  The boy gives warning something doth approach.
  What cursed foot wanders this way to-night
  To cross my obsequies and true love's rite?
  What, with a torch? Muffle me, night, awhile. [Retires.]

    Enter Romeo, and Balthasar with a torch, a mattock,
            and a crow of iron.

Rom. Give me that mattock and the wrenching iron.
  Hold, take this letter. Early in the morning
  See thou deliver it to my lord and father.
  Give me the light. Upon thy life I charge thee,
  Whate'er thou hearest or seest, stand all aloof
  And do not interrupt me in my course.
  Why I descend into this bed of death
  Is partly to behold my lady's face,
  But chiefly to take thence from her dead finger
  A precious ring- a ring that I must use
  In dear employment. Therefore hence, be gone.
  But if thou, jealous, dost return to pry
  In what I farther shall intend to do,
  By heaven, I will tear thee joint by joint
  And strew this hungry churchyard with thy limbs.

    The time and my intents are savage-wild,
    More fierce and more inexorable far
    Than empty tigers or the roaring sea.

  Bal. I will be gone, sir, and not trouble you.

  Rom. So shalt thou show me friendship. Take thou that.
    Live, and be prosperous; and farewell, good fellow.

  Bal. [aside] For all this same, I'll hide me hereabout.
    His looks I fear, and his intents I doubt. [Retires.]

  Rom. Thou detestable maw, thou womb of death,
    Gorg'd with the dearest morsel of the earth,
    Thus I enforce thy rotten jaws to open,
    And in despite I'll cram thee with more food.
                            Romeo opens the tomb.

  Par. This is that banish'd haughty Montague
    That murd'red my love's cousin- with which grief
    It is supposed the fair creature died-
    And here is come to do some villanous shame
    To the dead bodies. I will apprehend him.
    Stop thy unhallowed toil, vile Montague!
    Can vengeance be pursu'd further than death?
    Condemned villain, I do apprehend thee.
    Obey, and go with me; for thou must die.

  Rom. I must indeed; and therefore came I hither.
    Good gentle youth, tempt not a desp'rate man.
    Fly hence and leave me. Think upon these gone;
    Let them affright thee. I beseech thee, youth,

But not another sin upon my head
By urging me to fury. O, be gone!
By heaven, I love thee better than myself,
For I come hither arm'd against myself.
Stay not, be gone. Live, and hereafter say
A madman's mercy bid thee run away.

Par. I do defy thy, conjuration
  And apprehend thee for a felon here.

Rom. Wilt thou provoke me? Then have at thee, boy!
                    They fight.

Page. O Lord, they fight! I will go call the watch.
                    [Exit. Paris falls.]

Par. O, I am slain! If thou be merciful,
  Open the tomb, lay me with Juliet. [Dies.]

Rom. In faith, I will. Let me peruse this face.
  Mercutio's kinsman, noble County Paris!
  What said my man when my betossed soul
  Did not attend him as we rode? I think
  He told me Paris should have married Juliet.
  Said he not so? or did I dream it so?
  Or am I mad, hearing him talk of Juliet
  To think it was so? O, give me thy hand,
  One writ with me in sour misfortune's book!
  I'll bury thee in a triumphant grave.
  A grave? O, no, a lanthorn, slaught'red youth,
  For here lies Juliet, and her beauty makes
  This vault a feasting presence full of light.

Death, lie thou there, by a dead man interr'd.
                    [Lays him in the tomb.]
How oft when men are at the point of death
Have they been merry! which their keepers call
A lightning before death. O, how may I
Call this a lightning? O my love! my wife!
Death, that hath suck'd the honey of thy breath,
Hath had no power yet upon thy beauty.
Thou art not conquer'd. Beauty's ensign yet
Is crimson in thy lips and in thy cheeks,
And death's pale flag is not advanced there.
Tybalt, liest thou there in thy bloody sheet?
O, what more favour can I do to thee
Than with that hand that cut thy youth in twain
To sunder his that was thine enemy?
Forgive me, cousin.' Ah, dear Juliet,
Why art thou yet so fair? Shall I believe
That unsubstantial Death is amorous,
And that the lean abhorred monster keeps
Thee here in dark to be his paramour?
For fear of that I still will stay with thee
And never from this palace of dim night
Depart again. Here, here will I remain
With worms that are thy chambermaids. O, here
Will I set up my everlasting rest
And shake the yoke of inauspicious stars
From this world-wearied flesh. Eyes, look your last!
Arms, take your last embrace! and, lips, O you
The doors of breath, seal with a righteous kiss
A dateless bargain to engrossing death!
Come, bitter conduct; come, unsavoury guide!
Thou desperate pilot, now at once run on
The dashing rocks thy seasick weary bark!
Here's to my love! [Drinks.] O true apothecary!

Thy drugs are quick. Thus with a kiss I die. *Falls.*

Enter Friar [Laurence], with lanthorn, crow, and spade.

Friar. Saint Francis be my speed! how oft to-night
Have my old feet stumbled at graves! Who's there?

Bal. Here's one, a friend, and one that knows you well.

Friar. Bliss be upon you! Tell me, good my friend,
What torch is yond that vainly lends his light
To grubs and eyeless skulls? As I discern,
It burneth in the Capels' monument.

Bal. It doth so, holy sir; and there's my master,
One that you love.

Friar. Who is it?

Bal. Romeo.

Friar. How long hath he been there?

Bal. Full half an hour.

Friar. Go with me to the vault.

Bal. I dare not, sir.
My master knows not but I am gone hence,
And fearfully did menace me with death
If I did stay to look on his intents.

Friar. Stay then; I'll go alone. Fear comes upon me.
O, much I fear some ill unthrifty thing.

Bal. As I did sleep under this yew tree here,
I dreamt my master and another fought,
And that my master slew him.

Friar. Romeo!
Alack, alack, what blood is this which stains
The stony entrance of this sepulchre?
What mean these masterless and gory swords
 To lie discolour'd by this place of peace? [Enters the tomb.]
Romeo! O, pale! Who else? What, Paris too?
And steep'd in blood? Ah, what an unkind hour
Is guilty of this lamentable chance! The lady stirs.
                Juliet rises.

Jul. O comfortable friar! where is my lord?
I do remember well where I should be,
And there I am. Where is my Romeo?

Friar. I hear some noise. Lady, come from that nest
Of death, contagion, and unnatural sleep.
A greater power than we can contradict
Hath thwarted our intents. Come, come away.
Thy husband in thy bosom there lies dead;
And Paris too. Come, I'll dispose of thee
Among a sisterhood of holy nuns.
Stay not to question, for the watch is coming.
Come, go, good Juliet. I dare no longer stay.

Jul. Go, get thee hence, for I will not away.
                Exit [Friar].
What's here? A cup, clos'd in my true love's hand?
Poison, I see, hath been his timeless end.

O churl! drunk all, and left no friendly drop
To help me after? I will kiss thy lips.
Haply some poison yet doth hang on them
To make me die with a restorative. [Kisses him.]
Thy lips are warm!

Chief Watch. [within] Lead, boy. Which way?
Yea, noise? Then I'll be brief. O happy dagger!
                [Snatches Romeo's dagger.]
This is thy sheath; there rest, and let me die.
        She stabs herself and falls [on Romeo's body].

Enter [Paris's] Boy and Watch.

Boy. This is the place. There, where the torch doth burn.

  Chief Watch. 'the ground is bloody. Search about the churchyard.
  Go, some of you; whoe'er you find attach.
                   [Exeunt some of the Watch.]
Pitiful sight! here lies the County slain;
And Juliet bleeding, warm, and newly dead,
Who here hath lain this two days buried.
Go, tell the Prince; run to the Capulets;
Raise up the Montagues; some others search.
                 [Exeunt others of the Watch.]
We see the ground whereon these woes do lie,
But the true ground of all these piteous woes
We cannot without circumstance descry.

Enter [some of the Watch,] with Romeo's Man [Balthasar].

2. Watch. Here's Romeo's man. We found him in the churchyard.

Chief Watch. Hold him in safety till the Prince come hither.

Enter Friar [Laurence] and another Watchman.

3. Watch. Here is a friar that trembles, sighs, and weeps.
We took this mattock and this spade from him
As he was coming from this churchyard side.

Chief Watch. A great suspicion! Stay the friar too.

Enter the Prince [and Attendants].

Prince. What misadventure is so early up,
That calls our person from our morning rest?

Enter Capulet and his Wife [with others].

Cap. What should it be, that they so shriek abroad?

Wife. The people in the street cry 'Romeo,'
Some 'Juliet,' and some 'Paris'; and all run,
With open outcry, toward our monument.

Prince. What fear is this which startles in our ears?

Chief Watch. Sovereign, here lies the County Paris slain;
And Romeo dead; and Juliet, dead before,
Warm and new kill'd.

Prince. Search, seek, and know how this foul murder comes.

Chief Watch. Here is a friar, and slaughter'd Romeo's man,
  With instruments upon them fit to open
  These dead men's tombs.

Cap. O heavens! O wife, look how our daughter bleeds!
  This dagger hath mista'en, for, lo, his house
  Is empty on the back of Montague,
  And it missheathed in my daughter's bosom!

Wife. O me! this sight of death is as a bell
  That warns my old age to a sepulchre.

Enter Montague [and others].

Prince. Come, Montague; for thou art early up
  To see thy son and heir more early down.

Mon. Alas, my liege, my wife is dead to-night!
  Grief of my son's exile hath stopp'd her breath.
  What further woe conspires against mine age?

Prince. Look, and thou shalt see.

Mon. O thou untaught! what manners is in this,
  To press before thy father to a grave?

Prince. Seal up the mouth of outrage for a while,
  Till we can clear these ambiguities
  And know their spring, their head, their true descent;

And then will I be general of your woes
And lead you even to death. Meantime forbear,
And let mischance be slave to patience.
Bring forth the parties of suspicion.

Friar. I am the greatest, able to do least,
Yet most suspected, as the time and place
Doth make against me, of this direful murther;
And here I stand, both to impeach and purge
Myself condemned and myself excus'd.

Prince. Then say it once what thou dost know in this.

Friar. I will be brief, for my short date of breath
Is not so long as is a tedious tale.
Romeo, there dead, was husband to that Juliet;
And she, there dead, that Romeo's faithful wife.
I married them; and their stol'n marriage day
Was Tybalt's doomsday, whose untimely death
Banish'd the new-made bridegroom from this city;
For whom, and not for Tybalt, Juliet pin'd.
You, to remove that siege of grief from her,
Betroth'd and would have married her perforce
To County Paris. Then comes she to me
And with wild looks bid me devise some mean
To rid her from this second marriage,
Or in my cell there would she kill herself.
Then gave I her (so tutored by my art)
A sleeping potion; which so took effect
As I intended, for it wrought on her
The form of death. Meantime I writ to Romeo
That he should hither come as this dire night
To help to take her from her borrowed grave,

  Being the time the potion's force should cease.
  But he which bore my letter, Friar John,
  Was stay'd by accident, and yesternight
  Return'd my letter back. Then all alone
  At the prefixed hour of her waking
  Came I to take her from her kindred's vault;
  Meaning to keep her closely at my cell
  Till I conveniently could send to Romeo.
  But when I came, some minute ere the time
  Of her awaking, here untimely lay
  The noble Paris and true Romeo dead.
  She wakes; and I entreated her come forth
  And bear this work of heaven with patience;
  But then a noise did scare me from the tomb,
  And she, too desperate, would not go with me,
  But, as it seems, did violence on herself.
  All this I know, and to the marriage
  Her nurse is privy; and if aught in this
  Miscarried by my fault, let my old life
  Be sacrific'd, some hour before his time,
  Unto the rigour of severest law.

 Prince. We still have known thee for a holy man.
  Where's Romeo's man? What can he say in this?

 Bal. I brought my master news of Juliet's death;
  And then in post he came from Mantua
  To this same place, to this same monument.
  This letter he early bid me give his father,
  And threat'ned me with death, going in the vault,
  If I departed not and left him there.

Prince. Give me the letter. I will look on it.
Where is the County's page that rais'd the watch?
Sirrah, what made your master in this place?

Boy. He came with flowers to strew his lady's grave;
And bid me stand aloof, and so I did.
Anon comes one with light to ope the tomb;
And by-and-by my master drew on him;
And then I ran away to call the watch.

Prince. This letter doth make good the friar's words,
Their course of love, the tidings of her death;
And here he writes that he did buy a poison
Of a poor pothecary, and therewithal
Came to this vault to die, and lie with Juliet.
Where be these enemies? Capulet, Montage,
See what a scourge is laid upon your hate,
That heaven finds means to kill your joys with love!
And I, for winking at you, discords too,
Have lost a brace of kinsmen. All are punish'd.

Cap. O brother Montague, give me thy hand.
This is my daughter's jointure, for no more
Can I demand.

Mon. But I can give thee more;
For I will raise her Statue in pure gold,
That whiles Verona by that name is known,
There shall no figure at such rate be set
As that of true and faithful Juliet.

Cap. As rich shall Romeo's by his lady's lie-
Poor sacrifices of our enmity!

Prince. A glooming peace this morning with it brings.
The sun for sorrow will not show his head.
Go hence, to have more talk of these sad things;
Some shall be pardon'd, and some punished;
For never was a story of more woe
Than this of Juliet and her Romeo.
                              Exeunt omnes.

Act Five, Scene Three Summary

Melancholy Paris and his Page stand watch at Juliet's tomb with the goal that nobody will loot the vault. Romeo and Balthasar show up, and Paris attempts to limit Romeo, who is centered around breaking into the tomb. Paris perceives Romeo as the man who slaughtered Tybalt, and accepts that he has come to profane Juliet's cadaver. Their contention grows into a sword battle, and Romeo murders Paris. Paris' Page surges away to bring the City Watchmen.

Romeo opens the tomb and discovers Juliet's body. Naturally crushed, he sits beside his cherished and beverages the Apothecary's toxic substance, kisses Juliet, and afterward passes on. In the interim, Friar Laurence shows up at the Capulet tomb to discover Paris' body outside the entryway.

As arranged, the mixture wears off and Juliet stirs in the tomb, discovering Romeo's dead body adjacent to her.

At the point when she sees the toxic substance, she understands what has occurred. She kisses Romeo with the expectation that the toxic substance will murder her too, however it doesn't work. From outside the tomb, Friar Laurence asks Juliet to leave the vault and escape, however she decides to execute herself with Romeo's knife.

Before long, Prince Escalus shows up, joined by the City Watchmen and the patriarchs of the quarreling families. Master Montague reports that Lady Montague has kicked the bucket from a wrecked heart because of Romeo's expulsion. Monk Laurence then discloses what has befallen Romeo and Juliet, and Balthasar gives the Prince the letter from Romeo, which affirms the Friar's story.

To offer some kind of reparation for Juliet's demise, Lord Montague vows to raise a brilliant statue of her for all of Verona to respect. Not to be beaten, Capulet vows to do likewise for Romeo. The Prince parts of the bargains praising the finish of the fight, yet deploring the passings of the youthful sweethearts, asserting, "For never was an account of more trouble/Than this of Juliet and her Romeo" (5.3.308-9).

Act 5, Analysis

As the plot of Romeo and Juliet spirals to its distressed end, it is anything but difficult to overlook that the story happens over a couple of days. In any case, Romeo and Juliet are so sure of their affection that they decide to acknowledge passing as opposed to being isolated. As noted in the Analysis for Act 3, Romeo and Juliet develop significantly through the span of the play, and figure out how to acknowledge the heartbreaking edge of life more completely than their folks can.

Demise is the most unmistakable topic in Act 5, in spite of the fact that Shakespeare has foreshadowed the disastrous new development all through the play. Be that as it may, Shakespeare eventually outlines passing as a chivalrous decision. For instance, Romeo's in the end ends it all as a result of his enduring commitment to Juliet, which is a differentiation to the apprehensive inspirations for his suicide endeavor in Act 3. At the point when Romeo knows about Juliet's demise, he settles on a functioning decision, requesting Balthasar to set up a pony right away. Notwithstanding the edgy conditions, Romeo shows that he has gained from Juliet's forward arranging by buying the toxin before going to Verona. He needs to hold onto passing as Juliet has, and plans to take his life in a demonstration of solidarity with his adored.

At the point when Romeo purchases his toxin, Shakespeare portrays the scene as though Romeo were buying the toxic substance from Death himself - most remarkably in his depiction of the Apothecary: "Small were his looks. /Sharp wretchedness had worn him to the bones" (5.1.40-1). Emblematically, Romeo is effectively searching out death. Shakespeare shows that passing won't happen upon Romeo unprepared, however is happy to work in administration of the grief stricken youngster. Right now, adjusts Romeo to the old style original of the unfortunate legend who acknowledges his horrible destiny head on. Much in the manner that the characters in Richard III long for their destinies in the last demonstration of that play, Romeo additionally has a fantasy which foresees his destiny. He says, "I envisioned my woman came and discovered me dead" (5.1.6). The fantasy both anticipates the consummation and recommends that more noteworthy powers – maybe the "plague" that Mercutio attempted to deliver – have met up to guarantee a disastrous closure.

The occasions of Act 5 don't give an away from to the topic of whether Romeo and Juliet is a disaster of destiny. Rather, one could keep on argueing that the grievous closure is the consequence of individual choices - most prominently, Friar Laurence's entangled arrangement. The accomplishment of this arrangement is exceptionally dependent upon timing and condition. Imagine a scenario where Friar John had not been waylaid. Imagine a scenario where Romeo had shown up at the Capulet tomb two hours after the fact, or if Friar Laurence had shown up one hour sooner. Destiny isn't regularly so dependent upon human activities, which proposes that the most remarkable power grinding away in Romeo and Juliet is really the brain science of the characters. The vulnerability in these last scenes makes the play less traditionally disastrous but then progressively one of a kind for not being completely adjusted any one structure.

Monk Laurence keeps on upholding for control in the last scenes of Romeo and Juliet. Numerous researchers accept that Shakespeare implied for his crowd to remove the message that an absence of balance is the explanation behind Romeo and Juliet's destruction. Some accept that Romeo and Juliet acted too rapidly and strongly on their energetic energy, and permitted it to expend them. In any case, this ethical perusing feels like a distortion, and overlooks the complexities of their adoration. Rather, alert is seemingly progressively appropriate to Romeo and Juliet's families, who have permitted their fight to gain out of power.

Shakespeare likewise utilizes the repetitive theme of gold and silver to scrutinize the whimsicalness of the quarreling grown-ups. Gold keeps on speaking to riches and envy, the indecencies that keep Romeo and Juliet separated. At the point when Romeo pays the Apothecary in gold, he comments, "There is thy gold - more awful toxin to men's spirits" (5.1.79). Gold, as an image, underlies the family quarreling. Considerably after Romeo and Juliet are dead and their families probably consent to harmony, they despite everything attempt to exceed each other by making dedicatory gold statues. Romeo perceives the influence of gold but then revokes it, permitting Shakespeare to make a differentiation between the sorts of individuals who esteem cash and the individuals who worth genuine affection.

In spite of the fact that demise is vital in Act 5, love is as yet a significant topic too. Specifically, Shakespeare utilizes sensual imagery, particularly in the demise scene. Romeo drinks from a goblet, a cup formed like a lady's middle. Then Juliet says, "O glad blade,/This is thy sheath! There rust, and let me pass on" (5.3.169). The blade she talks about is Romeo's, in this way featuring the sexual hints of her declaration. Moreover, Shakespeare utilizes "pass on" questionably. In Shakespeare's time, "To bite the dust" could either allude to genuine demise or sex. In this manner, even at the finish of the play, the crowd could decipher Juliet's last articulation as her aim to end it all or her longing to draw in with Romeo explicitly. The sexual idea of their relationship remains as a glaring difference to Juliet's masterminded union with Paris, which depends on legislative issues and insatiability, not love.

It is critical to take note of that in Romeo and Juliet, the ethical shows of marriage, religion, and family are totally recolored by human indiscretion. The virtue of Romeo and Juliet's affection has no spot in a world loaded up with moral defilement. Shakespeare outlines Romeo and Juliet's 'story of misfortune' as a disastrous exercise to their families, which has an effect on the crowd also. The Montagues and Capulets accommodate over a mutual feeling of misfortune, as opposed to good or cultural weight. The crowd leaves from the play trusting that these families have gained from the unfortunate occasions.

Be that as it may, one investigation of Friar Laurence proposes the issue is more muddled. As noted beforehand, the Friar is to a greater degree a keen legislator than a devout priest. He controls an affection and-demise circumstance for political harmony. He does this by making an elixir that has exceptional forces - as though he is playing God. By giving Juliet the mixture, Friar Laurence places her in a Christ-like situation (since the two of them 'passed on' and afterward were restored from a tomb). Minister Laurence's disappointment could be perused as an analysis of hubris, just as discipline for a natural man attempting to establish divine force - subsequently strengthening the common idea of the play.

THE END

Made in United States
Troutdale, OR
03/08/2024